The Promise

TESSA VIDAL

LOVEBIRD PRESS

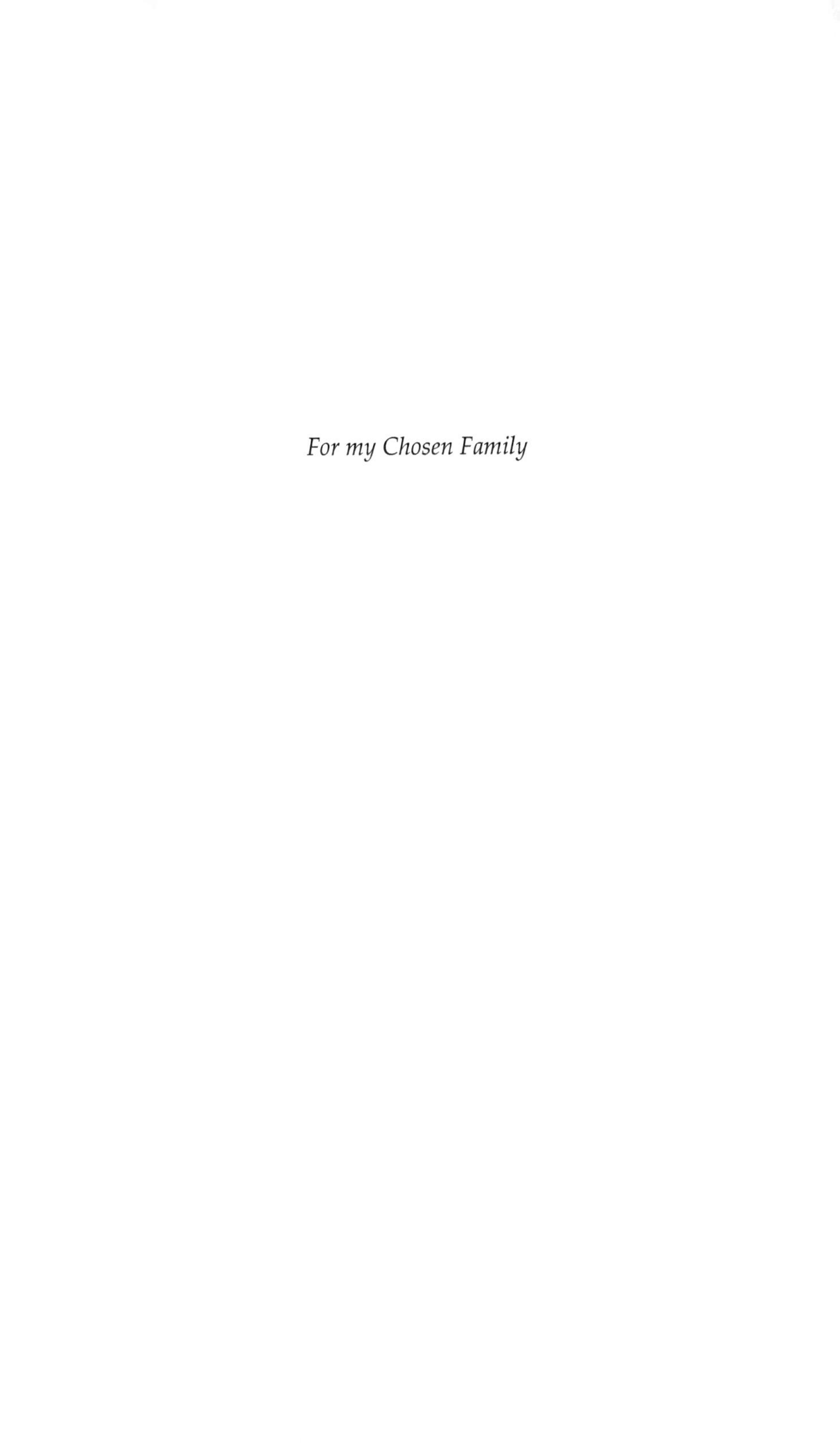

For my Chosen Family

"ARE YOU SCARED? You know, enlisting in the marines?" Ashley asked, tightening her grip on my hand as we strolled around Lake Johnson. I stopped in my tracks and turned to face her, our eyes locking.

"What do you think?" I sighed, then she pulled me into her chest and kissed the tip of my nose. "I'm not scared of joining the service, Ashley. Losing you forever is my deepest fear."

Ashley's soft curves trembled, and I felt her heart beating against mine as our hug deepened.

Ashley had been my first at just about everything. For the last two years of high school we'd been inseparable, unable to be apart for any stretch of time. The thin, gorgeous eighteen-year-old had stolen my heart at the beginning of our junior year, and the night we graduated we'd skipped the parties and headed to her family's beach house on the outer banks. There we shared our true feelings for the first time, both with words and our bodies.

"I love you so much, Carly." Ashley's velvety voice trembled, and her grip on me grew stronger. "How am I going to survive without you?"

A tear slid down my cheek, because the same fear filled me with an ache I'd never experienced before. I felt Ashley's fingers on the back of my neck, and seconds later, she was staring into my eyes again.

"Let's run away." I whispered, the sound of frogs and cicadas nearly drowning out my voice.

The pressure behind my eyes burned, because I wanted nothing more than to be by her side, always. Her thumb swiped at the tears now flowing down my cheeks. Ashley's full lips inched closer to my mouth, and seconds later her lips crashed against mine, taking my breath away. Searing heat surged through me, and my legs trembled as I tried to maintain my balance. My friends had all complained about having sex with their boyfriends, how all the hype around their first time had only led to disappointment and guilt.

Making love to Ashley was different, and not just because we were both girls. We'd been each other's first, and the emotional and physical bond between us had only deepened with every encounter. The feel of her silky skin was intoxicating, and combined with the love I felt, I couldn't imagine ever being with another woman.

There had been many sleepless nights where I lay awake, wondering what it would be like to live with Ashley, and to wake up in her arms every morning. She was my everything.

"Please," I moaned, breaking the kiss, "you know I want to be with you, more than anything else in the world."

"Then let's do it. Between our savings and graduation gifts we can afford to strike out on our own." Ashley's voice cracked. I placed my hands against her shoulders and gently pushed her away.

"You know we can't do that." I sniffed, then backed out of

her arms and began pacing, hugging myself. "Not that I don't want to, but…"

"I can still go to college." Ashley interrupted. "We couldn't afford Harvard medical school, but we…"

"I have to join the service. And as much as I care for you, Ashley, being a surgeon has been your lifelong dream. Graduating from Harvard would open up almost any door for you." Without thinking, I placed a lock of my chestnut hair in my mouth, a habit I'd broken in elementary school.

Ashley abruptly turned away and stalked a few feet ahead. That was when I noticed her shoulders shaking, and my resolve threatened to break. As much as she wanted to be a doctor, how could I let go of this love so soon? I sighed, then picked up a stone from the path and skimmed it across the water.

"Damn it," I whispered. "Why do we have to choose?"

"I'm sorry," Ashley murmured. "I shouldn't be pressuring you like this. You're heading to San Diego for basic training in three days, and I'm off to Florida tomorrow. You have your whole life ahead of you, and so do I." She sighed, then wrapped her arm around my waist and we both stared across the lake. I could hear honking in the distance, and moments later a flock of geese descended. They'd always frightened me, especially when they defended their nests. But that fear didn't even come close to the terror I felt now at losing Ashley.

"Does it really have to end?" Ashley murmured. "Can't we…"

"I don't want it to, Ashley. But my parents want me to serve four years in the marines, and then Dad wants me to join the family business. You know, that's where my parents met, in the service. Shit." I muttered, stepping away and kicking a stone into the water, provoking a flutter of wings from the geese now swimming a few feet away.

"And I'll be in med school. Never-ending school." Ashley

sighed, both of us dreading our new lives, yet excited to start it. "We can't… we just can't make it, not with all these obstacles in front of us. Long distance relationships always fail."

I strolled over to where Ashley stood, and placed my hands on her forearms. "You are my first love, Ashley, and no one will ever take that away from me."

Her blue eyes were wet, and she glanced up to the darkening sky, and gulped. "Let's make a promise."

My breath hitched, and I nodded for her to continue.

"Both of us have a bunch of things happening to us over the next few years, so yeah, a long-distance relationship isn't going to…" Ashley turned her head and swiped at her eyes, then met my gaze again. "In ten years' time, if we both are still single, let's meet at our high school reunion and maybe we can…"

"Pick up from where we're leaving it now?" I whispered, a flicker of hope radiating throughout my chest. Then, it dawned on me that the likelihood of that happening was close to zero.

Ashley nodded, her face softening while her cheeks burned red. It felt like someone had punched me in the stomach, and I'd do anything in the world to see Ashley's teeth split into a smile.

"I promise you, Ashley, in ten years we will be together, though I don't know how I'm going to wait so long."

"This isn't over, Carly, and it never will be. I promise you will always have my heart, and if I have to wait until…"

"Stop." I reached up and laid a finger across her full lips. "I can't bear this anymore." A sob threatened, and I didn't want to make our goodbye more painful than it was.

"I love you, Carly." Ashley kissed the tip of my finger, then brushed her lips across mine.

"Oh Ashley, I love you too." I whispered, then we both turned toward the lake and watched the water turn orange from the setting sun. "Don't you ever forget that."

CHAPTER

One

ASHLEY

"ARE you excited to meet your new colleagues?" The woman from human resources asked in the cramped and nearly airless elevator. Her demeanor was cool and professional. It was packed, the doors opening on every floor, letting people in and out. A gurney took up half the space, forcing the two of us against the rear wall.

I knew I should answer quickly, laced with my best sincere smile. But the ball of anxiety spinning in my gut made that difficult to do. It was my first day of work at the UNC Rex Hospital in the ER. I'd moved home to Raleigh from Boston to make a fresh start in my hometown. It was comforting to see familiar places, but starting a new job was stressful, especially after being gone for so long. Twenty years in Boston, the last four spent nursing at Tufts Medical Center. Finally, my lips stretched across my face in a semblance of a smile, and I managed a small nod.

"Well, the staff are looking forward to meeting you, and they will put you to work right away. The emergency room is always hopping. Never a dull moment." A phone vibrated in her pocket. She pulled it out, raised an eyebrow, and scowled.

"I thought I'd have time to show you around the floor, but an emergency of my own has come up." She said, and I must have made a face. "Don't worry, I won't leave you stranded. I have someone who will work with you for the next two weeks to make sure you learn the correct procedures." Her eyes never connected with mine, and the ball of anxiety bounced up to my rib cage.

Human resources was on the fourteenth floor, so by the time the elevator doors slid open on the first, I was ready to race out of the cramped space. I'd never been claustrophobic before, but my nerves were on edge. It felt like day one of school again, not knowing anyone or anything. I glanced at the woman's name tag. LaTrice Wiggins. I knew the woman meant well, but her stiff demeanor left something to be desired. Oh, and her perfume was a powdery rose that overwhelmed the small space we were in.

It took every ounce of self-control not to run out of the elevator and straight through the sliding doors on the other side of the ER. I waited for LaTrice to exit first, and when I stepped on to the floor I was amazed at the calm. This was a gigantic hospital, and I expected it to be a madhouse from the get go. Instead, the staff patiently went about their business. A few of them were standing together, obviously gossiping, but when they saw LaTrice, they parted in a hurry. Apparently, she was someone they didn't want to cross.

"Ashley?" LaTrice's grin was gone, and she was glaring at her watch.

"I'm sorry, what were you saying?" My cheeks burned, caught not paying attention.

"That's okay, but I need to be on the ninth floor immediately. Come with me." She hurried toward the nurses' station in the middle of the ward.

"Nancy, where's Mark?" She asked a nurse, an older woman with a neutral smile she assumed as soon as she noticed LaTrice heading her way.

"Mark's at the pharmacy, but he should be back any minute. Would you like me to page him?" She said, picking up the phone.

"No, that won't be necessary. Nancy, this is Ashley James. She's moved here from Boston and today is her first day on staff. I have to leave Ashley here with you. Something has come up, or I'd stay with her myself. Mark is expecting her, so let him know Ashley is here as soon as he returns to the floor." She turned without another word and jogged toward the elevator. Nancy's mouth opened to reply, but LaTrice was already gone. Her eyebrow lifted, and she shook her head.

"It's a pleasure to meet you. They scheduled me for my break five minutes ago. If you don't mind I'm going to let you sit in an empty office until Mark returns." She reached under the counter and pulled out a thick binder, and handed it to me. It was a manual of procedures, and must have weighed ten pounds. "This way." She led me down the hall and deposited me in a small gray room with a single window.

"I'm sorry, but you've arrived when it's relatively calm. I need to take my break now, otherwise, well, you know what it's like." She shook her head, then shut the door behind her.

I sat at a plain metal desk. There were no pictures or decorations, only the familiar smell of disinfectant. I opened the manual, prepared to at least give it a cursory glance, but my thoughts wandered to why I was here in the first place.

"You've come full circle, home again." I whispered, then turned in the chair and looked out the window. A mixture of medical students and staff were strolling up and down the sidewalk. A few in pairs, but most had their heads down, hurrying to their destinations. Since I was new, I had few responsibilities, and I envied them their sense of purpose. The most pressing thing on my to-do list was finding a reputable hairdresser, who hopefully could wax my legs, too. My strawberry-blonde hair was so thick, I had to have it thinned out every few months, or it grew into a towering mess of split ends.

I'd arrived in Raleigh less than a week ago, escaping the chill of another Boston winter, or that's what I told myself. I'd spent twenty years up north, only coming home for sporadic visits to my Aunt Dotty. She'd graciously taken me in until I could find my own apartment. My parents had moved to Florida three years ago, so she was my only family here. Since I hadn't maintained contact with anyone else in Raleigh, it felt like a fresh start.

I heard a thump outside the door and my knee jumped and hit the bottom of the desk. I flipped through the manual, keeping one eye on the door, hoping I appeared to be busy studying. Footsteps hurried away, and I sighed with relief, glad I wasn't caught daydreaming.

"No more dating doctors. You are to come to the hospital and leave alone." I spoke aloud, a faint echo filling the empty space.

I drummed my pink fingernails on the desk, impatient for this Mark person to put me to work. The longer I was alone, the more I could think of my humiliation. A few months ago I'd been jilted at the altar by Dr. Grayson Trainor, abandoned for a younger surgical intern. It was for the best, since oddly enough, I hadn't missed him. On paper, he'd torn my heart to shreds. But what I didn't tell anyone, was that instead of pain, I felt relief. Like missing an airplane at the last minute and discovering it had crashed into the ocean later that day. I thought I'd been in love with Grayson. He was supremely confident, and cocky, a top doctor in a crowded city teeming with ambitious doctors. In the rearview mirror though, he left me empty, devoid of passion. I'd only known true love once, but that was like a teenage dream, one you would wake up from, and despite closing your eyes over and over again, it's lost forever.

I'd loved my job, and despite the chilly winter, Boston was an amazing place to live. What drove me away were the gossips. They were thrilled to whisper about it all over Tufts Medical. It was humiliating, and Grayson only gave me a curt apology, never minding the trauma he had put me through. The pediatric ward I truly loved went from being the perfect work environment to a nightmare overnight. After a month of sideways glances and whispered speculation, I turned in my notice.

"You just had to shit where you eat, didn't you?" I reminded myself for the umpteenth time. This job would be different. Come to work, do my job, then go home. My heart was permanently encased in surgical steel, and if I had anything to say about it, it would stay that way.

The door burst open, and a man in scrubs stepped in, hands on hips and a broad smile plastered on his face.

"Hi! I'm Mark. You must be Ashley. Welcome to insanity." His hands spoke as loudly as his words. He had flaming red hair and freckles sprinkled across his nose. Mark's enthusiasm was infectious, and I returned his grin with a genuine one of my own.

"Nice to meet you, Mark." I started to stand, but he gestured for me to stay seated.

"Sit, sit. It's quiet on the floor, which scares me. Whenever we get a lull, something insane happens." He sat across from me on the other side of the desk. "I was informed by her highness, LaTrice, that I am to be your mentor for the next two weeks. She's someone to be avoided at all costs, if you know what's best for you." He winked.

"Well, she does have a certain, um..." I started, then he burst into laughter.

"Oh my gawd, that look on your face is priceless. You're definitely going to fit in. Yes, a stick resides deep in her ass. Oh, and don't ever get trapped in an elevator with her. That godawful perfume would gag a maggot." He slapped his thigh and giggled, and moments later I giggled, too. Looked like my new job wouldn't be as boring as I thought. Boston was a crazy city, so I thought little old Raleigh would be a snore fest.

"Before I show you around, tell me a little about yourself. You'd better do it now, because at the drop of a hat this place can turn into a madhouse. Where did you work last?" Mark's bright blue eyes twinkled.

"I moved here from Boston. Worked at Tufts, in pediatrics." My gut clenched again, but this time it was a pang of regret. Had I made the right choice moving to Raleigh? There were other hospitals in Boston where I could've moved on with my life without coworkers knowing about my humiliation.

"Strange, you don't have an accent. I love Boston, oh and the beaches at Provincetown are beautiful, but I had the hardest time understanding anyone." Mark opened the office door and peeked out, checking to see if the floor was doing okay. When he closed it, I answered.

"I'm actually from Raleigh, moved away twenty years ago. I guess that explains the lack of an accent. And yes, I used to go to the beach..." my mouth snapped shut while thoughts of long weekends with Grayson at his condo on Cape Cod flooded my mind. Status and luxury were my rewards for being with my ex, and though I missed that part, I certainly didn't miss him. Until I got to know Mark better, I'd keep my history to myself.

"Ah, sounds like a woman with a past. Tell me later over a cocktail. So, you come from pediatrics. Have you worked in ER before?" Mark asked, eyebrows coming together. He was probably nervous about training a total newbie.

"Yes, I worked in the ER for a few years, then I transferred to pediatrics for a change of pace. It can get pretty crazy there too." I said, then the door swung open. A young nurse with wide eyes interrupted us.

"Mark, there's been a multi-car pileup on New Bern Avenue. Get out here, the first ambulance is pulling up now." Adrenaline surged through my limbs and we both got to our feet. Mark held out his arm for me to go first.

"Welcome to the ER."

———

I leaned against the nurses' station and dabbed my brow with a tissue. Despite the chaos I felt fantastic. Work was exactly what I wanted, keeping my hands busy and my mind on anything but myself. Now that things had calmed down a little, they had me behind the desk until I knew more about how the department operated. At least, until the next big emergency.

"I brought you some lunch. Hope you like egg salad sandwiches. Let's go back to that office. Normally we'd eat in the cafeteria, but I want to make sure we're close by in case anything comes up." Mark grinned and walked away. I followed behind, trying to keep up with his quick steps. Damn, if it was like this everyday, I wouldn't have time to miss the slower pace of pediatrics.

"So how are you holding up?" He asked as I opened the white paper bag. I pulled out a soggy egg salad sandwich and was overwhelmed by hunger. I'd been too nervous about the new job to eat breakfast this morning.

"That was something else. I haven't been this busy in

years." I mumbled, then scarfed down a quarter of the sandwich in one bite.

"You're going to be just fine. I can tell you've done this before. You were a big help, trust me. And hey, we've only got six more hours to go!" Mark laughed, then started on his own meal. A couple of minutes later he put down his food and spoke.

"For the rest of the shift you'll be working triage. I know you still don't know all the procedures, but it will help you learn the department better than anything else. Just check people in, and figure out the top priority cases. If you have any questions, page me. I'm sorry to eat and run, but I want to make sure Dr. Spruill has everything he needs." Mark winked, his sly grin giving his game away.

"Which one was Dr. Spruill?" I asked innocently, knowing exactly who the hot doctor was. I might be off the dating scene, but he was a looker I'd immediately noticed as we took care of patients together. Blood rushed to Mark's face.

"Only the most delicious doctor in the hospital. Of course, he doesn't even know I'm alive. But I can dream." Mark sighed, then threw the remnants of his lunch in the trash. I bit my tongue, wanting to warn him away from nurse/doctor relationships. Grayson's face flashed in my mind, then I thought once again how my life would be so much better if I'd never pursued him.

"What's wrong? You look like you've seen a ghost." Mark asked, then stood. No way I'd let him in on my office romance humiliation. I needed to be professional, even if he wasn't.

"First day jitters I guess."

———

"My daughter thinks I'm having a heart attack."

"Let's see what is going on, Mr…" I asked, wanting to hear him say his name to figure out how alert he still was. When I saw the chart, warning bells went off inside my head. He was older, late fifties I guessed. The man looked familiar, and his commanding voice made me regret eating that soggy sandwich for lunch.

"Poindexter. Grayson Poindexter. My daughter and I were inspecting a property we might buy, and I felt a sharp pain in my chest. I think it's indigestion. Can't stand doctors, but Carly insisted she bring me in." The man had a domineering attitude that I was starting to remember from years ago. More importantly, I recognized his name.

"Dr. Spruill will examine you, but before that you're getting an EKG." I said, then an older male nurse rolled the machine in.

"Perfect timing." I murmured, then I handed him the chart and beat a hasty retreat. Not only was the old man having a heart problem, but my own was suddenly pounding. The urge to hide in that gray, empty office overwhelmed me, but I hurried to the nurses' station instead. As I circled the corner, I saw a statuesque woman standing at the nurses' station with her back to me. Her dark brown hair was cut in a smart bob, and even though her hands were talking as loud as she was, through her panic she sounded like a woman comfortable giving orders. She was speaking to a flustered nurse who was trying to calm her down.

"Is he okay? Dad's always been like Ironman. What's happening? Shit, I need to call Mom." The woman reached into her back pocket for her phone.

"Damn it." I muttered. That velvety drawl was so familiar, because it was the voice in my teenage dreams that haunted me to this day.

I caught a glimpse of her face, and in an instant her chestnut eyes locked with mine. She had a confident air about her that suggested arrogance, someone used to getting her own way. She cocked her head, then her perfectly arched eyebrows drew together. Without a second thought I turned on my heels and jogged around the corner, then leaned against the wall, breathless.

"It can't be her. My first day back and it's fucking Carly." I whispered, shaking my head. No way she would be here on the first day of my new job.Those sparkling brown eyes and sharp cheekbones were ingrained in my mind, never to be forgotten. And damn, she was a knockout. Father Time had been good to my ex-girlfriend. Gone was the skinny teenager I once loved. She'd filled out, and her ample curves were evident under her tight red suit. I felt a flush spreading across my chest, and I wondered if I was going to hyperventilate. Carly was standing only a few feet away, and instead of being elated, I wanted a hole in the ground to open up and swallow me.

I wrapped my arms around my chest and struggled to control my breathing. If this could have happened a few months from now, the timing would be perfect, but not on my first day of work. And especially not so soon after my last disastrous attempt at a relationship. An orderly pushing a patient in a wheelchair gave me an odd look as she passed.

"She probably doesn't remember you, or she's seeing some-one. Nobody that drop-dead gorgeous is single, plus, you are not searching for a relationship. Pull yourself together, Ashley. This is your first day of work, so don't mess it up." I muttered, then straightened my back and strolled toward the nurses' station.

Carly was pacing in front of the desk, her cellphone pressed against her ear. I walked behind the counter and was about to hide in a supply closet when I heard my name called.

"Ashley?" Carly's voice rang out over the low roar of the

ER. The skin on my arms pebbled at the sound, and my heart leapt into my throat. Damn it, I couldn't have a panic attack on the first day of work. I guessed there was no escaping the inevitable. Turning around, I tentatively gazed into those dark eyes that occasionally haunted my thoughts to this day. But they were fantasies, not reality. There was no way she could be the same girl I once loved after all these years.

"May I help you?" I replied, my voice scarcely above a whisper.

"It's me, Carly. Carly Poindexter." She opened her Louis Vuitton purse and dropped her phone inside. "My father is here, and I think he's having a heart attack. You are Ashley James, right?" She cocked her head and looked me dead in the eyes. Jesus, they were so sexy and dark, the color of chocolate. My knees shook, and I placed my hand on the desk for balance. I didn't want to deal with this. I opened my mouth to deny it, then noticed another nurse staring at us with curious eyes.

"Yes, I'm Ashley James." I choked out, feeling my knees tremble. What the hell? I couldn't even act normal around her.

"Don't you remember me? We both attended the same school, we, um…" Carly said, and I saw a flush creeping up from the collar of her blouse to her sharp cheekbones. My heart raced, and I felt beads of sweat forming on my upper lip. What the hell could I say? How did I escape her intense gaze without looking like a total idiot? Images of me standing alone in front of hopeful and confused guests at my wedding flashed through my mind. I didn't want to hurt her feelings, but I'd had enough rejection lately to last an entire lifetime.

"Sorry, I can't talk right now."

CHAPTER

Two

CARLY

"DAMN IT CARLY, I will not get in the back of an ambulance, so don't call one." Dad barked, collapsing against the wall of the commercial building we were inspecting. He'd clutched his chest and gasped for air moments ago, and I'd immediately grabbed my phone.

"Dad, this could be serious." I jammed it back in my purse. "Fine. If you're going to be stubborn, just get in the car and I'll drive you home. Mom, can look after you. But don't you die on me, or she'll never speak to me again." I took Dad's elbow in my hand, which he shrugged off. Then he straightened up and gingerly walked across the parking lot, at one point falling ever so slightly into a parked car. Once he was inside, he sat back in the seat and gasped for air. He was pasty looking, and his forehead was covered in a sheen of sweat. I backed out of the lot and ran the stop sign at the end of the block.

"What the hell are you doing? You'll get us killed!" Dad yelled, then gripped the oh-shit handle above the door. I said nothing and raced through every stop sign and traffic light on Capitol Boulevard, barrelling toward UNC Rex Hospital.

"Carly. Where are you driving me? You're going in the wrong direction." Dad panted, finally sounding like a man in distress.

"The hospital. Where the hell else would I take you?" I yelled, then instantly regretted it. Now that Dad knew where we were going, he'd make it harder for us to get there. I pulled into the parking lot of a grocery store then turned to face him.

"Listen, old man. You're going to the hospital whether you like it or not. Got it?" I could feel my pulse throbbing in my ears, and wondered if I was as difficult as my father with other people.

Dad reached for the door handle.

"Oh no you don't, you son of a bitch!" I stomped on the gas and pulled back onto the street, before Dad could open the door, narrowly missing two cars as I raced through a red light.

My father was a royal pain in the ass, but I'd rather have him alive than dead.

———

"Carter, don't talk to Mom yet. Dad's always been healthy, never had any issues with his heart. If it's serious, I'll call you." I paced in front of the nurses' station. My brother was freaking out almost as bad as I was, but I knew it wouldn't do any good to get Mom upset, unless it was a dire situation.

"I'm calling Erik and asking if he can fill in for me. I'll be right there." His voice rose with every word, and then I heard the sound of breaking glass.

"What the hell was that?" Shit, I shouldn't have called him either. Between Carter and Mom, the entire hospital would be in an uproar in a matter of seconds.

"I fucking dropped a glass. I'm calling Erik now." He disconnected the call before I could stop him.

"Carter? Damn it." I was about to call him back when I saw a face I hadn't seen in years.

Ashley.

It couldn't be her. Maybe it was her doppelgänger, one of those lookalikes everyone was supposed to have. Of course, twenty years had passed, and there were subtle differences. There was no way it could be her, but if it was, I had to speak. The only woman I'd ever loved was walking in the opposite direction, and I'd dreamt of seeing her again for two decades.

"Ashley?"

The woman stopped in her tracks, her back stiff, then slowly turned on her heels. Those bright green eyes met mine, and for a moment I couldn't breathe. Images of her soft curves and angelic face flushed with excitement while we made love flashed in my head. If it wasn't Ashley, it was her identical twin.

"May I help you?" She asked, then shifted her gaze from me to the floor. That was her voice, I knew it. Our friends used to tease her that she could make a living as a phone sex operator, because of how seductive she sounded.

"It's me, Carly. Carly Poindexter. My father is here, and I think he's having a heart attack. You are Ashley James, right?" My heart galloped in my chest, and for a second I wondered if I'd be joining Dad in the examination room. Ashley recognized me, I knew she did. Shit, I'd had so many conversations with her in my head over the years. When I was in the Marines she was by my side the entire time, even if it was only in my imagination. The memory of her smooth and sensual voice made the loneliness of the service bearable, and those months in Iraq less horrifying.

"Yes, I'm Ashley James." She placed her hand against the desk and peeked up again, not entirely meeting my gaze. I stepped forward, wanting to close the gap between us.

"Don't you remember me? We went to the same school, we, um…" I started, but I saw Ashley closing herself off, like an invisible forcefield slamming down between us.

"Sorry, I can't talk right now." Ashley's emerald eyes avoided mine

This couldn't be happening. How could she not want to talk, or even worse, what if she didn't remember me at all? Was Ashley hit on the head or something? Maybe did too many drugs at Harvard? Harvard, yes. I knew she went there, at the same time as I joined the Marines.

"You went to Harvard. I remember you were going to Florida, and then Harvard after graduation. I enlisted in the Marines. Dad made me… shit. My old man. Can you help me with him?" Fuck. If she was deliberately ignoring me, I'd at least get her to speak with me about Dad. Hell, what was I thinking, using my sick father to get at my high school crush at a time like this?

"Grayson Poindexter, yes, I've already seen him. He should be with Dr. Spruill right now." Ashley said, then she grabbed a chart off the counter and glanced through it. She turned the sheets of paper over with her long tapered fingers, and then I noticed something. Her hands were trembling.

Ashley remembered me, she had to.

"Why don't I go check on him now. He was about to get an EKG when I left him. It shouldn't be long. Heart patients are always seen first." Ashley smiled, then placed the clipboard under her arm. She began walking off and then she turned around, took a deep breath and locked her hypnotic eyes with mine.

"Yes, I attended Harvard." She ran her fingers through her strawberry-blonde hair, then continued. "Let me check on your father now. Maybe we can chat a little more when we know how he's doing."

———

I paced the waiting room, resisting the urge to scream. My father could be dying, and the only woman I'd ever loved barely recognized me. Between these two events happening simultaneously, I thought I'd combust, my heart being shredded by the most important people I'd known in my entire life.

How could Ashley forget about me? And if she remembered, how come she'd pretended she didn't? Was she a closet case? That last evening we spent together still brought on an attack of the blues whenever I'd had too much to drink. It was a rare occurrence when I allowed that far-off memory to invade my brain, because it was so painful. When she twisted the door handle to let herself out of the car for the final time, I wanted to pull her back inside and floor it. Harvard and the Marines could go to hell.

Pressure built behind my eyes, heat spreading to my cheeks. I knew I would blubber like a baby any minute now if I didn't calm down. I'd cried the night Ashley and I separated, torn apart by family obligations and an unfair world, and it hadn't happened since then. I placed my hands against my eyes, hoping to stem the tide. Moments later I heard footsteps, then felt a hand on my shoulder. When I looked up, Ashley was staring down at me. She raised one eyebrow the same as she used to do, then a genuine smile spread across her face. I always wondered how people could do that, only lifting one eyebrow at a time. She sat next to me and spoke in low measured tones.

"Your father is with Dr. Spruill right now. Other than that, I don't have any information. I am the triage nurse, so all I did was check him in and make sure he was seen immediately. As soon as I know anything else, I'll tell you." Ashley placed her hands on the arms of the chair to push herself up and without thinking I seized her tiny wrist. Ashley sucked in her breath, then fell back in the seat. When I let go, she pressed her full lips together and opened her mouth. Initially, nothing came out, and I could see she was struggling to find the right words.

"You shocked me, that's all. I'm sorry Carly, but so much time has passed. Yes, I remember you, but… an awful lot has happened over the years. I don't know what else to say, but I apologize for not…" She stopped, then stood up, and this time I kept my hands to myself. Ashley glanced around the waiting room, then crouched down in front of me.

"This is not the time nor the place to talk about our past, about what might or might not have happened all those years ago. What I can say is that your father is receiving excellent care. I promise you that." She glanced at her watch. "I have to go upstairs and will be passing the cafeteria. Can I get you a cup of coffee perhaps, or a soda?" Warmth radiated from her now, instead of the cold woman I'd first encountered. I wanted to speak, but something held me back. I shook my head and crossed my arms over my chest. Ashley walked halfway across the waiting room, then stopped. It looked like she would turn around, but then she kept going.

Ashley was still proud and regal, with curves in all the right places. Underneath her scrubs I could tell little had changed since we'd parted. But, she was right. Dad was sick, and this wasn't the right moment to stroll down memory lane.

My jaw clenched, frustration seeping into my bones. Why now? Couldn't I have run into her at a bar, or at the grocery store? This was torture, seeing Ashley after all these years while my father might be fighting for his life.

"No matter what happens, you and I need to talk, Ashley."

———

"Your father is asking for you. Follow me."

An older woman led me to a semi-private room where I found Ashley and the doctor, both with their arms crossed, and that wide-eyed gaze I'd come to recognize when Dad was tearing someone a new asshole. He stopped harassing them and turned his vitriol on me.

"I told you I would be all right. It wasn't a damned heart attack. This was the stupidest waste of time I've..."

I cut him off before his language became more exotic.

"Dad, if it had been you would've died. What the hell did you want me to do? Let you croak in the parking lot?" My pulse raced, and for the second time that day I wondered if I would be admitted to the hospital too.

"Your daughter did the right thing, Mr. Poindexter. Plus, you aren't out of the woods healthwise. You have an ulcer, and I believe it's a result of stress. I am instructing you to cut down your workload, optimally taking a few days off. Maybe you could have your daughter help you with..." Dr. Spruill began, then Dad shouted.

"Yeah, right, me take time off? No one in my real-estate firm is competent enough to do the shit I do. The business would go under in less than a week." Dad snarled, then glared at me with scarcely hidden contempt.

Fuck you, Dad.

The words were on my tongue, but I controlled myself. Ashley stared at me with what looked like pity, with a dash of horror thrown in. Damn it all, why did my father have to say this crap in front of her?

The old man had never given me any credit for the effort I put into making the company the success it was. Probably because I'm a woman. This had been happening since day one, and the thought of walking away from the family busi-ness was always with me. I'd started my own real estate business on the side, hoping to back out of my father's firm gracefully, but I still worked with him part-time. Damn it, now I'd have to be with him more often to make sure he didn't overdo it.

Silence settled over us for a few moments, and finally, Dr. Spruill spoke, "Mr. Poindexter, I will have the nurse release you. She will give you information about a healthier eating plan, stress reduction techniques, and a prescription. I want to reiterate something though, and I'm being deadly serious. You must work on your stress levels. This ulcer is only the beginning of potential health problems, and if you don't address it now, you could very well end up back here with…"

"Yeah, yeah, yeah. Get me out of here, Carly," Dad barked, then swung his legs over the side of the bed. "Fetch that stuff from the nurse while I get dressed."

Ashley and the doctor left, and I trotted behind them, grateful to escape the room. Once we were in the hallway, both spun around and faced me.

"You've got your hands full there. Please, do whatever you can to settle him down." The doctor gave me a rueful smile, and looked at Ashley. "This is your first day here, right?" Ashley nodded. "Welcome to the wonderful world of the ER. Never a dull moment." With that, he hurried off.

Ashley shrugged her shoulders and leaned against the wall, then she hung her head and laughed.

"Your father hasn't changed one bit. I'm sorry."

"Yeah. He's something else... Hey! You do remember stuff about us." I stood next to her on the wall, pressing my shoulder against hers. I wanted to wrap my arms around her tiny waist and pull her in tight. The feeling overwhelmed me, and I couldn't look Ashley in the eye. No one had ever replaced her in my heart, despite years of solitude and filling my bed with nameless women. If she still affected me this way, I needed to act on it, otherwise I'd always wonder what could have happened if I'd only spoken up.

"Can I take you to lunch tomorrow? If you're not busy or anything? I mean, I would like us to catch up. Nothing serious, no pressure. All I want is…"

"That would be nice." Ashley murmured, then I felt her shoulder leaning heavier into mine. I turned my head in her direction, and that goofy half-smile, the one she used to hide her feelings with, was there. Ashley had always been shy, and getting her to open up, to laugh and be herself was my mission in life when we were in high school. My heart lurched, and I wanted to run my fingers through her wavy blonde hair. I remembered doing that, always rubbing on her, touching her when I thought no one was looking.

"Carly! C'mon, get me out of here." Dad said, standing in the doorway. Ashley pushed herself off the wall and jogged to the nurses' station. She found the papers we needed, and hurried back, handing Dad his release forms. Dad snatched them out of her hand and raced toward the exit.

"I got your number off his papers. I'll text you tomorrow." Ashley turned, flashed her brilliant white smile at me one last time, and rushed away.

I dashed off a text to Carter telling him Dad was heading home, that there was nothing to worry about, then he barked at me, "Carly! Jesus Christ, come on."

I shook off Dad's words and followed him out the exit. As I hustled after him, a bolt of anxiety shot through me, making my stomach clench, and I stopped for a moment, provoking a glare from the Old Man. A disquieting thought passed through my mind.

Had Ashley ever dreamed about me the way I did her?

"WANT to eat with me in the cafeteria?" Mark asked as we walked off the floor of the ER. I was torn. It would be so much easier to text Carly and tell her I couldn't make it for lunch. Mark was safe, a pleasant distraction from the crazy world of the ER. But, a promise was a promise, and I wouldn't let Carly down. Plus, I was curious about how her life had been since we parted all those years ago.

"I wish I could, but I've already got plans." I hurried out before Mark could try to persuade me otherwise. Carly and I were meeting at The Raleigh Times, an old restaurant that had existed since the earth cooled. It was a neutral place to meet up, and it had been years since I'd last eaten their fantastic Reuben sandwich.

"This would be so much easier if we'd met six months from now." I said aloud as I entered the parking deck and hustled toward my car. This wasn't part of my plans, meeting up with Carly so soon after moving back to Raleigh. Carly was my high school girlfriend, that was all, nothing more, nothing less. I needed to look toward the future, and dating wasn't a part of it, even if Carly was still easy on the eye. But I'd be damned if I would give in to it. I'd had enough romance and rejection to last a lifetime, thank you very much.

I let myself in the car and was about to pull out of the deck when an image of our first kiss flashed through my mind. She'd always been the popular girl in school, self-assured and used to getting her own way. When she showed an interest in me, I'd been shocked. Why was the most popular girl in our class suddenly following me around, determined to hang out with me? I was the geeky girl whose face was always in a book.

It all started when a teacher asked me to help Carly with her classwork. We met in the library every day for a week, and to her credit, she was perfectly polite.This made me believe Carly was just being friendly, that she truly was only looking to bring up her grades.

Then, she asked me to go out with her on a date. Back then I wasn't comfortable with my sexuality, but something about her intrigued me. She was the most popular girl in our class, and I couldn't understand why she'd ask shy, nerdy, me out on a date. Carly took me to a dance at the LGBTQ center, and she'd been the perfect date, holding my hand and making me feel like the most important girl on earth. And when we slow-danced together, I totally swooned in her arms.

For the next month we dated, and Carly kept her hands to herself, until I began to wonder why she wasn't making any advances. So, I made the first move, asking Carly to take me to her room when her folks weren't at home. It was scary, because I'd never been with a woman or a man before, but at the time I was totally consumed by Carly, and couldn't imagine anyone else being my first.

Carly wasted no time, pushing me flat on my back against her bed, and covering my trembling body with her own. The heat I felt when her lips touched mine for the first time was something I'd never forgotten. Then she used her lips on my neck, and around my ears, and soon I was panting for more, though I wasn't sure what that would entail.

I loved it.

Neither of us knew what we were doing, instinct driving our lips to touch, and for our hands to fumble around awkwardly. Despite our lack of skills in the lovemaking department, she was an amazing lover, and I'd compared every man or woman to her ever since.

"Stop thinking about it now." I muttered to myself, and pulled onto the busy street. "Be positive." Carly was part of my past, and it might be worthwhile to catch up. I could use a friend, and she was probably only interested in that and nothing more. Reading anything else into this lunch date with a high school girlfriend would be hazardous to my mental health.

———

Carly's chic presence always took over entire rooms, commanding the attention of everyone there. Standing on the sidewalk outside of The Raleigh Times, she seemed like the only person there, despite people maneuvering around her. She was tall, and wore a red skirt and a white blouse that made her tanned skin glow. Damn it, why did Carly have to be my exact type? I tripped when we finally were face-to-face, and for a second I thought I'd end up on the ground. Instead, Carly caught me by the shoulders with a laugh.

"Thanks for coming." Carly grinned, then instead of sticking her hand out to shake mine, she pulled me into an embrace. The feel of her body pressed so close transported me back to those long afternoons we'd spent in her bedroom after school. Heat radiated between my legs, then Carly's arms tightened. This was no quick hug between friends. The urge to melt into her slender arms was overwhelming, but I knew nothing good could come of it.

Carly always had the ability to make me do whatever she wanted, whether it was skipping a class, or taking me to her bed. Now my body betrayed me, and I felt the old familiar excitement building inside, so I pushed back just the tiniest bit, enough for Carly to know to disengage. When she pulled away, I glanced at my watch.

"I don't have too long before I have to be back at work. Let's grab a table." I opened the door to the restaurant, grateful to see there wasn't a line to be seated. Moments later, a waiter led us to a booth in the back. Carly took the seat facing the dining room, while I was confronted with only her. I knew twenty years had passed, but aside from a few lines around her eyes, her face was almost the same. I noticed a few flecks of gray in her hair, and I found it sexy. If anything, Carly looked hotter than she did back then.

How long has it been since you had mind-blowing sex, Ashley? Or any sex at all?

"The special is the Reuben, and I highly recommend a bowl of the matzo ball soup too." The waiter interrupted my trance, and I sighed with relief. Looking up, I noticed Carly's gaze planted squarely on my face. A shiver coursed through me, and I turned away.

"That, um, that sounds great. I'll have both." I said, then Carly nodded. The waiter didn't see her nod and glanced at the tables surrounding us. I could see his impatience building, so I gave Carly a little kick under the table.

"I'll have what she's having." Carly's eyes never left mine as she spoke. I felt blood rushing up my neck, so I picked up the napkin and spread it across my lap, anything to avoid staring into her intense dark eyes. The waiter scurried away, and for a moment I wished he'd come back, to act as a buffer of some sort between us. How Carly still made me feel so uncomfortable, so turned on after all these years was mystifying.

"Penny for your thoughts?" Carly said, her grin fading as I looked into her eyes once more. I obviously wasn't going to tell her I wanted to leap over the table and kiss her the way we used to kiss, before we went our separate ways. Instead, I thought back to the questions I'd rehearsed last night in front of the mirror. I didn't want her to get the wrong idea. Nothing too intimate, but enough to let Carly know I was curious about her life since we'd parted.

"Well, I was wondering about what you've been up to since we last saw each other. You went into the Marines, right?" I asked, then Carly looked away for a second, and ran her tapered fingers through her hair. She frowned, and I wondered if perhaps her life hadn't gone as well as she expected.

Before I could say something else, you know, to change the subject and lighten the mood, she spoke, "Yeah, at the end of our last summer together I went to San Diego for boot camp. It was the most miserable I've ever been in my life. I wanted to be anywhere but there, but you know, sometimes you've got to do things you don't like. I'd like to think I made the best of it." Carly's eyes blanked for a moment. "Then, they sent me to Iraq. I'd only signed up for four years, but the war extended my stay by an extra fifteen months. It would have been longer, but I was injured, so they let me out."

"I hope it was nothing serious? What did you do next?" I imagined the worst, then briefly wondered how I would have reacted if we'd stayed in touch. How would I have felt finding out Carly was in a war zone, injured?

"Nothing too bad, hit by shrapnel. I have a scar on my back from it, but the war itself damaged my head more than the physical stuff. Thank God I wasn't on the front lines, because the boys had it worse. Seeing your friends explode in front of you will shake your belief in, well, just about anything." Carly's eyes got smaller, and I felt my body responding to her words. Now I really wanted to wrap my arms around her. I struggled for the words to distract her, but she continued before I could spit something out.

"I came home and Dad put me to work. He actually cried when he saw my scar, and he apologized for insisting I join the Marines. Mom and him met while in the service during peace-time, and he never expected me to end up on the other side of the planet being shot at." Carly said, and I noticed shadows under her eyes that makeup couldn't completely hide. "Dad decided not to let my baby brother join the service after what happened to me, and Carter's been grateful ever since." Carly picked up her napkin and dabbed at her eyes. "You've seen my father at his worst, but he was at his best then. He knew I needed to keep busy, to put that time behind me. His answer to everything is work. At first I helped out around the office, you know, filing, that kind of stuff. Then, he taught me how to open my own real-estate business, which I run when I'm not working for him. Now, when I look back at that period of my life, I am damned grateful to him for keeping me sane. Dad didn't give me the time to feel sorry for myself." Carly picked up her glass of water and sipped it, glancing away. Carly never liked to talk about herself from what I remembered. So why was she sharing so much? It wasn't like we knew each other that well anymore. This conversation was so heavy, not at all what I imagined it would be.

"What about you? How did Harvard treat you?" As soon as she asked me about school, the waiter brought our soup. I was embarrassed about that period of my life, and wondered if I should come clean about it. I looked up to see Carly waiting for me, the matzo ball soup untouched. Well, if she could be that open about her past, so could I.

"They threw me out." I said, then picked up my spoon and played with the soup, feeling more vulnerable than I thought I would.

"What are you talking about? I mean, you were the valedictorian of our class. I don't get it. What happened?" Carly said, her eyes wide.

"My roommate's boyfriend happened. He came on to me, and when I didn't respond to his advances, he got even by framing me for academic dishonesty. That's a fancy way of saying he accused me of cheating. I was tossed out, and after a year of waiting tables, I decided if I couldn't go to Harvard, I could at least get more education. I put myself through state college, and though I didn't become a doctor like I'd planned, I still got my nursing degree." I shrugged my shoulders. "Life doesn't always go the way we think it will, does it?"

Moments later, our sandwiches arrived, and for a few minutes, we said nothing as we consumed our lunch. I'd told no one about Harvard, about the embarrassment I felt at being kicked out of school. Why I'd felt the urge to share it with Carly, I didn't know. I snuck a few glances at her while we were eating. She still had that self-assuredness that compelled me to share everything with her, no matter how much it made me cringe. She was the only person who'd ever made me feel so open, comfortable.

"It's amazing you pulled yourself together after that." Carly said, interrupting my inner monologue. "So what brought you home, back to Raleigh?"

Damn it, the one question I didn't want to answer, especially to her. I thought back to the night before when I'd paced my room wondering what I'd say if she asked me about my move home. Yes, I'd stick with that explanation. The truth would be a little too revealing.

"The thought of another Boston winter was killing me. My

parents live in Florida now, and I didn't want to go that far south, so this seemed like a good place to settle." I took a bite of my sandwich, unable to look her in the eye. For some reason the Reuben didn't taste as good as I remembered.

"What's the real reason you moved back?" Carly said, then bit her lower lip.

Damn it, why did she do this to me? I put the remnants of the sandwich on the plate and pushed it aside. All thoughts of discretion and common sense left me.

"I was engaged to be married to a doctor at the hospital I worked at. His name is Frank, and he's a surgeon at Tufts. We'd planned the perfect wedding on the Cape, and most of the staff we worked with were invited to attend. We were going to honeymoon in Barbados, and we'd already decided to buy a summer place in the Berkshires. I showed up in my Vera Wang gown, ready to say I do. He didn't." I bit off the last two words, surprised I still felt bitter. The affection I'd felt for Frank wasn't love. It had been about status, and a reprieve from the loneliness which had crept up over the years.

"Frank went on the honeymoon, but instead of me he took a younger surgical intern named Brandy. I hope they enjoyed themselves." I chuckled, surprising myself. Carly's mouth was open, and instead of being embarrassed, I felt a weight lifted from my shoulders.

"Honestly, I would have stayed in Boston if not for the gossip. Every day I'd go into work to find another rumor circulating throughout the hospital. Finally, I'd had enough and put in my notice."

"Damn, that's harsh. Count your lucky stars, Ashley. You can do a lot better than that." Carly pushed her plate aside and leaned back in the booth. "I've avoided love, never wanted to put myself through the shit I see my friends putting up with. What I realized after you left, I'd never found the right woman.

I mean, at the time, hell, I'm…" Her words stumbled, and a blush came to her cheeks. Carly's nails tapped on the table, a staccato rhythm that gave away her embarrassment.

Suddenly, her face underwent a transformation, her full lips curving up slightly. "What do you remember about us? You know, about our relationship?" Carly asked, then leaned forward waiting for my answer.

What the hell could I say? Yes, I'd spent a lot of time wondering how it would have worked out if I hadn't moved away to school, and if she hadn't joined the Marines. Carly was the only woman who was able to get me to escape my head, and the insecurities, and make me feel… important? When she'd said she loved me the night we said goodbye, her words wrapped around me in an almost physical sensation, caressed and encircled by raw emotion. But after Frank, and the humiliation of being dumped in the most visible way possible, I wasn't setting myself up for more disappointment.

"We were kids, discovering ourselves for the first time. I'll always remember it, in a good way."

Carly's face fell, the smile fading from her lips. Damn it, now I wanted to take it back, tell her how I'd really felt all those years ago. If only she knew how I'd spent years going on date after date, and being miserably disappointed in every man or woman I went out with. No one compared to her memory, but that was all she was now. Too much time had passed for Carly to be anything else, and I wasn't emotionally prepared for her to be anything more than a friend.

"So now I'm staying with my Aunt Dotty until I find my own place." I said, breaking the awkward silence threatening us again. Carly's face lit up, and something in my gut loosened. I didn't like seeing her sad, especially if I'd caused it.

"Well, I'm just the woman you need to see. I'm a realtor, and I've got lots of places I could show you. Do you want to live downtown? I've got places in every price range, and I'd love to help you out." Carly said, nearly bouncing in her seat.

Damn, the energy she had reminded me so much of when we were teenagers. I had the urge to stroke the length of her neck, and run my fingers through the back of her hair. In that moment I remembered exactly how she'd felt holding me, her full lips covering mine. This effect she had on me wasn't good, and I felt sweat sliding down my sides.

"Are you ready for your check?" The waiter didn't wait for our answer and placed it on the table before rushing to the next one.

Thank God.

"I've got this." Carly said, snatching it up before I could grab it.

"You don't have to do—" I started, before she interrupted.

"Yes, I do, but you have to do me a favor." Carly said, light dancing in her eyes. Damn, her eyelashes were still so thick, and it didn't look like she had mascara on. "Ashley...? You still there?" Fuck, she'd caught me staring.

I shook my head and laughed. "Sorry, I have a lot on my mind with my new job, trying to find a place to live. You know." I shrugged my shoulders, hoping to play it off.

"Well, I want you to come and see me. I've got time later this afternoon to show you a few places. I mean, you do need a place to live. What time do you get off? Work, I mean, when do you get off work?" She dipped her head down while keeping her gaze focused on me. I blurted out the time before I could think of an excuse not to.

"5:30."

"Excellent." Carly glanced at her watch, then grabbed her purse and stood. "Sorry to eat and run, but I'll miss an appointment if I don't scoot." She placed her business card on the table in front of me, then laid her hand on my shoulder. "See you later tonight."

"Yeah, I'll come by after work." I responded weakly, then Carly's face broke into that huge smile I'd never forgotten, the one that made me squirm inside. Damn it. Moments later I heard the bell on the door of the restaurant ring as she let herself out.

"What the hell are you doing?" I grumbled, clenching my fists, then I stood and chased her out the door. When I got to the sidewalk I scanned the street, hoping to catch her before she got away. I wanted to cancel, tell her I couldn't make it, but I was too late.

"Carly, why do you do this to me?" I muttered, then hurried toward my car. When I got in I peered into the rear-view mirror, surprised to find myself grinning from ear to ear. She used to do this to me all the time when we were teenagers. Carly always found a way of inviting herself over to my house, but making it seem like it was my idea, or how we'd suddenly be kissing and it was almost always me who initiated it.

"Establish boundaries. Don't give her the impression you want anything more than friendship. Oh, and a place to live."

Carly wanted to catch up, that was all. She didn't say anything to make me think otherwise, and had behaved like an old friend, that's all. Though something in her eyes made me think she wanted something more.

It was the way she looked at me with that self-assured grin and confident attitude. Demanding the attention of everyone in a room, whether they wanted to give it or not. She was the eternal spirited girl, used to getting whatever she wanted, all while looking as innocent as an angel.

"I'm not giving in this time, Carly." I whispered, then put my car in gear and headed back to the hospital.

"CARLY, YOUR FOUR O'CLOCK APPOINTMENT CANCELLED." The receptionist poked her head through the door to say, then hustled back to her desk.

"I forgot I had one." I mumbled, and leaned back in the chair. My normal, bland world had faded away as soon as I'd laid eyes on Ashley. Seeing her had provoked major butterfly action in my gut—something I hadn't felt for anyone since we parted twenty years ago. That was cause for concern. Since she left all those years ago, I'd avoided relationships, preferring string-free passion. Dating was a sport for me, and I didn't want more than simple flings. Also, I could count on one hand the women who'd turned me down. Let's just say that I nearly always bedded any woman I desired.

"Simple, casual sex is what it's supposed to be, not this crap." I said aloud, grateful Dad wasn't here to see me in this state. As soon as I'd seen Ashley in the ER, I was lost again in those feelings I'd done my best to forget about. No one had ever broken through the cage I kept my heart locked up in.

I remembered the first day of my senior year in high school, which was the first time we'd met. The catholic school we went to made girls wear the least attractive uniform possible, a plaid skirt and a boring white shirt. Despite the efforts of the nuns, Ashley's beauty shone through. We had just one class together, but the only thing I could focus on the entire day was her. I learned her name when the teacher called on her, and for the rest of the day and throughout the night it echoed in my head.

Ashley Ashley Ashley Ashley Ashley Ashley

I tried to make eye contact with her during class, but she kept her gaze on her notes. For the entire fifty minutes of boring Latin she'd avoided my stares, despite my willing her mentally to look in my direction. Hell, I thought I even prayed for her to look at me. I was used to getting what I wanted, and it only spurred me on to make her my friend, and hopefully more.

I'd never been a quitter. Getting what I wanted was ingrained in my psyche. Not only was I stubborn, I was also infinitely patient when pursuing a goal. The way I got to Ashley the first time was by deliberately flunking a Latin test. I'd always gotten good grades which baffled my teacher, so she asked Ashley to help me with my classwork. She was the new kid, and she made excellent grades, so I figured she'd pair us together. Ashley would make a new friend, and help me get my grades up. At the time I was only guessing this strategy would work, but my instincts were spot on.

The third time we met in the library to study together was when I made my first move. The moment she laid her books down next to mine, the air in the room shifted, becoming electric. I'd looked up to her and smiled, gratified to see a blush creeping up her neck until her cheeks flushed pink. Ashley pulled out her notes from class, but I had no use for them and laid my hand on hers for a brief moment, then pulled it away.

"We are here to study, right?" Ashley stuttered, her bright green eyes growing wide.

"What is something you've never told a soul about?" I asked, delighted to see the effect it had on her. Ashley's eyes scanned the room. We were sitting in the back of the stacks at a table reserved for studying. There was no one else around.

"Why are you asking me that? Aren't we supposed to be conjugating Latin verbs?" Ashley whispered.

"Come on, I'll tell you a secret if you share one with me." I leaned into her arm as I said it, wanting to put her at ease.

"If it'll make you want to study, then… fine. I count stuff in my head all the time."

"What do you mean?" I asked.

"Like, if I'm walking to class, I count all of my steps in my head, or if I'm eating, I count how many times I chew my food. I know it's strange, but…" Ashley shrugged, then turned and gazed into my eyes. "Your turn."

My eyes dropped to her full pink lips, and the urge to cover them with my own struck me. I gripped the sides of my chair to keep my hands to myself. Unable to think of anything to confess, my mouth stayed shut. Finally, Ashley elbowed me in the side, and grinned.

"C'mon, fair's fair. Tell me a secret."

"Okay, um…" I wracked my brain for something. I'd only asked her for a secret to get her to talk. It never occured to me that I'd need to confess something too.

"Whenever I read a book, this is in private of course, I act out the scenes, speaking the different parts aloud like I'm on stage, or in a movie. I use different voices and mannerisms for each character." I blushed, but didn't know why. It wasn't like I told her that I masturbated almost every single day with a vibrator I'd bought in secret. That was a pervy secret I'd take to my grave.

————

"Carly, what the hell is happening with the Blankenship deal?" Dad barged into my office, startling me from my memories. He perched on the edge of my desk, frowning. My father was in a mood, and I wished he'd go away.

"Dad, I sent the owner of the apartments an offer, the exact one you told me to. I still haven't heard from him." I replied, inwardly cringing, because I knew what would happen next.

"Seth is a friend of the family." Dad bellowed, then hit the top of the desk with his fist. "He's also one of our best clients. He wants to buy that property, and he's got more than enough money to make the owner a deal he can't refuse. Call him, go see him in person, I don't care. Make this deal happen, or I'll be very disappointed in you. Again." He said the last word through clenched teeth, then stalked out of my office in search of someone else to harass.

Fuck my life.

Dad had a talent for making me feel pathetic. Here I was boasting to myself about getting anything or anyone I wanted, and he had the power to make me feel like I was a stupid kid. If only he believed in me, trusted that I knew what I was doing. It wasn't like I didn't want us to succeed. The commission on this deal alone would make me a huge chunk of change. Screw it, focus on what you really want.

Ashley.

I glanced at my watch. She'd be here in a few minutes, and I hoped Dad would make an early night of it. I wanted nothing to spoil my time with Ashley, but if anyone could, it would be him. I'd put a folder together with different condos for sale, hoping I'd get to show her a few in person. Perhaps I could take her out for a drink afterward? Maybe, if I played my cards right, she'd let me hold her again, kiss her like I did the very first time?

————

"You have the entire basement to yourself?" Ashley asked as I led her down the stairs. I'd told her we were going to play video games, and maybe we would, eventually. But she was giving off vibes, and if I played my cards right, she'd end up in my bed.

"Yeah, my brother's at boarding school, so most of the time it's all mine."

I realized I'd somehow have to walk her through the TV room, which had the video games prominently displayed, in order to get her to the bedroom. That might not prove to be easy.

"Oh cool, you get to play on a large screen TV?" Ashley gushed, and started toward the sofa in front of the television.

"It's pretty cool, but I want to show you something else first." I grabbed her by the elbow and steered her down the hallway to my bedroom. Finally, I'd see if what I was feeling for Ashley was mutual. I took a deep breath and opened the bedroom door. I wasn't going to let fear stop me, though I knew the consequences could be harsh. What if she wasn't into women? Would she tell the entire school? My blood pumped faster, adrenaline coursing through my veins. Ashley stood in front of my bed, one eyebrow raised. At that moment I knew this was right.

"What are you doing?" Ashley placed shaking hands on my shoulders as if she wanted to push me back. I placed my hands on her shoulders and pushed ever so slightly until the backs of her knees were against the edge of the mattress.

"I'm doing what you want, what I've wanted since I first laid eyes on you Ashley."

One final push and she fell back against the mattress and I covered her with my body. Gazing into her eyes, I gave her one last chance to say no.

"Stop me now if you don't want this."

Her innocent face gave the faintest of nods, and moments later my lips crashed into hers. The jolt of her soft mouth pressed against mine made me forget anything else existed. I wasn't sure what to do, and let instinct guide me, though I was fairly sure I needed to keep all the action above the neck, though the feel of her breasts heaving underneath me was driving me crazy. I licked her lips, urging them to open, and when our tongues first touched, a groan rumbled through me, and she whimpered in response. My panties were soaked, and I could feel something inside me throbbing. I'd never felt such passion before, and it was so intense I thought I'd pass out.

"What are you doing to me? Oh God, Carly, I've wanted this since the day we first met." Ashley said as she broke away from our first kiss. Her hand reached out and grasped the back of my head, then pulled my face back toward hers.

———

"Carly," the receptionist poked her head through the door. "Ashley James is here to see you." She held the door open as Ashley walked in, then she shut it behind her. She stood in front of my desk, not saying anything, her green eyes dancing around my office. My cheeks warmed, and I realized I had to break the silence before it became overwhelming.

"So, this is where the magic happens." I laughed awkwardly, standing up. I didn't know whether to hug her, shake her hand, or pull her into my arms and kiss her the way I used to do. Instead of making a fool of myself, I gestured toward the seat in front of the desk. Then Dad poked his head through the door. He took a long look at Ashley, then at me.

"You're bringing the hospital to me now?" He scowled. I shook my head, hating every second of Dad's scorn.

Ashley's mouth dropped open, then she spoke, "No worries Mr. Poindexter. I'm here to find a place to live." Ashley glanced in my direction.

I was about to say something I'd regret, but the emerald green of her eyes stilled my tongue. I looked up to see Dad smiling for a change.

"Good, good. We have excellent properties for you to choose from, and the best prices in the city. Oh, Carly, remember what I told you about the Blankenship deal. I need it taken care of pronto." Dad said, then shut the door quietly as he left. Whenever money was being exchanged, he switched from being a devil to an angel, lickety split.

Ashley laughed, then bit her lip to quiet it.

"As you see, he hasn't changed a bit." I guffawed, then moments later both of us were holding our sides, unable to contain ourselves. It felt so fucking awesome, like we were teenagers pulling one over on our folks again, breaking curfew, or sneaking a kiss goodbye. Her laughter was like gold, and then it struck me that this was the first time I'd heard her really laugh since she'd re-entered my life. I'd give anything to keep Ashley this way, carefree, playful and happy.

Moments later though, Ashley sobered up and a look of purpose replaced her smile.

"So, what do you have to show me?"

I opened the folder on my desk and spread the different brochures in front of her, deliberately keeping a specific listing on top of the others.

"You didn't give me an idea of the area you want to live in, so I've got a few properties in mind. Are you looking to buy or rent? Did you know what part of the city you want to live in? Or did you want to look a little further out, like in Wake Forest, or Durham?" I asked.

"I'd rather be close to work, so downtown would be perfect. I hate driving, so someplace close enough I could catch the bus, perhaps? Oh, and I still don't know if I want to stay in Raleigh permanently, so I think a rental would work best." Ashley picked up the brochure I'd laid on top. I had to look away, so she couldn't see the look of disappointment I felt when she said she wanted to rent. I wasn't stupid, and I knew enough time had passed that maybe she wasn't attracted to me anymore, but I didn't like the sound of her leaving again. Damn it, I wanted a chance to discover if the way I felt was real, not some stupid fantasy.

"Why don't we look at some of the rentals in person? The brochures don't really do them justice, know what I mean?" I said.

"Sure, as long as you don't mind driving. So much has changed around here. I almost got lost on the way to your office." Ashley grinned, and my heart flipped in my chest.

"Pick out the ones you're interested in while I grab the master keys from the back." I stood, and when I passed behind her, I couldn't help myself and squeezed her shoulder. Ashley's back stiffened for a moment, then she relaxed. My heart started beating again, and I hustled out of the office. When I closed the door I fell against the wall, regretting that slip. I didn't want to scare her off, and moving too fast was the easiest way to do just that.

"Keep your cool Carly, don't lose control." I whispered, then glanced up to see the receptionist eyeing me with a raised brow.

What the hell was wrong with me? Just being close to her made me crazy, losing every ounce of self-control I possessed. I pushed myself off the wall and ran down the hallway to get the keys out of the closet where we had them hanging on hooks. I raced back, then realized I'd be out of breath and I needed to chill out for a moment. Once I got my breathing under control, I let myself back into the office.

"See any apartments you're dying to look at?" I grinned, hoping she'd picked the one on top.

"Yes, I think I'm interested in one of these." I took the brochures from her hand and bit my lip to keep from smiling.

"Your wish is my command. Let's go."

———

"I love this place." Ashley breathed, her footsteps echoing on the hardwood floors. Her eyes were glued to the balcony overlooking Fayetteville Street. She slid open the screen door and stepped outside. Dusk was approaching, and the sky was streaked with orange and purple clouds. I stood next to her, resisting the urge to put my arm around her waist.

"Look down. Everyone on the street is so tiny from up here." I said, then noticed her gripping the railing tight. "Are you nervous about heights?"

"Oh, no. This view, wow. It's incredible. I really missed Raleigh. Why the hell did I stay away for so long?" She murmured, shaking her head.

I've been wondering the same thing.

"You can be at the hospital in ten minutes depending on traffic. If you don't want to drive, you can catch the bus two blocks away at Moore Square. The laundry room is at the end of the hallway, and there's a gym on the first floor. It's a happy place. Most of our tenants have been here for a long time. The only reason this unit opened up is the previous tenant got married and moved away. She'd been here for seven years if I remember correctly." I realized I was babbling and shut my trap. Let the surroundings sell her on the place.

Ashley had always been slow to warm up to things. When we first started hanging out, she'd been painfully quiet, but then slowly she'd come out of her shell. Once comfortable, Ashley would run her mouth, desperate to tell me her secrets, or talk about the weird insecurities we all had, but never felt comfortable sharing. I wanted that Ashley back, and the only way it would happen was for her to come to me.

"I'll take it." Ashley leaned into my shoulder as we stood against the railing of the balcony. I barely controlled the urge to jump up and down.

"Excellent decision. You're gonna love it here. Let's run back to my office, sign the lease and I'll give you the keys. You can move in as soon as you want." I said, wanting to grab her by the waist, spin her around and enfold her in my arms. Instead, I pushed myself off the railing and walked inside. When I turned around to see if she was following, Ashley was less than a foot behind me, and we nearly collided. She backed up half-a-step, and that sexy blush started all over again, working its way up from her neck. Then she stunned me by reaching out and placing her hand on my shoulder.

"Since you bought me lunch, can I buy you dinner?" Ashley murmured, a small smile slowly stretching across her face. My mouth opened to reply, but nothing came out.

"Shit, I'm sorry, you've probably got other plans." She looked down at the floor and then started to walk around me toward the door. I reached out in the nick of time and grabbed her elbow.

"No, no no, I don't have any plans. I'd love to have dinner. We can go to Beasley's, they've got great fried chicken, and it's just down the street. I can show you around the neighborhood and stuff." I held my breath, not sure why, since she was the one who'd asked me out. Ashley's eyes locked with mine, and my legs felt weak.

Finally, she answered. "Let's go. I'm famished."

CHAPTER
Five

ASHLEY

"SIGN HERE, AND HERE." Carly said, then laid the keys to my new apartment next to my hand. I picked them up, feeling a twinge of panic. Locked into a lease for a year, a commitment to stay in Raleigh for at least that length of time. Stuffing them in my pocket, I looked up to see Carly's huge sparkling grin, and for a moment I felt something I hadn't in a long time: hope. Maybe, just maybe, the dreams I'd had over the years about me and her could come true.

Tearing my eyes away from hers, they dragged down her body, which despite her curves, was very trim. Carly's white blouse stretched over her breasts, and then her stomach flattened out before hitting the top button of her perfectly fitted red slacks. Carly managed to appear both professional and alluring at the same time.

"Ashley? You okay?" Caught staring, I felt blood rushing to my face. I stood, grabbed the keys and backed away from the desk. Endorphins raced through my body, reacting to the unfamiliar giddy lust Carly was provoking in me. I wracked my brain for something to say, and settled on the truth. Well, minus the lustful thoughts.

"Sorry, I guess I'm going to be in Raleigh for a minimum of a year now. I never thought it would be home again. Kinda scary to tell you the truth." I shook my head, wondering why I'd told her that. It had always been like this with Carly, a special magic she had to extract every private thought in my head.

"Well, maybe that's not such a bad thing. Actually, it makes me want to celebrate. Ready for dinner?" Carly came around the desk and rubbed my lower back, the heat of her hand soothing, almost hypnotic, like her velvety, alto voice. I could feel our off-the-charts chemistry rising to an incendiary level. A groan worked its way up my throat, and I felt myself getting wet from her touch. I coughed and backed away.

"Definitely. I've eaten nothing since lunch and I'm starving. I'll take my car and follow along behind you." I said, then raced out the door before she noticed what her hands did to me. Carly's touch drove me crazy, and her fingers could persuade me to do things I wasn't sure I was ready for.

When I sat my car, it struck me that it had been months, hell, almost a year since I'd last had sex—with Frank, of course— and what I didn't admit at that time was how I occasionally fantasized about other men and women to enjoy it. I'd give credit where credit was due; Frank wasn't a bad lover. What had been missing was the deep connection I longed for, but could never quite manage with him. At the time I wrote it off to premarital jitters, or a fear of commitment. Maybe there was something more to it than I thought.

A horn beeped. Carly waved as she pulled her cherry-red Jaguar out of the lot. I drove behind her, and while sitting at a red light, it dawned on me that when I'd fantasized about other people while with Frank, most of the time it was the sensual and enigmatic woman I was taking to dinner. Carly inspired more than physical desire, though, and that scared me more than anything else.

———

"The veggie sandwich is wonderful, and of course they are famous for their fried chicken and honey." Carly said as we opened our menus. The atmosphere was funky and eclectic, though Carly's taste in food surprised me. I thought she was into fitness and eating healthily.

"I'm surprised you'd like fried chicken and burgers, because it's obvious you're into your health, and I thought you'd be counting calories or eating low-carb." I asked, unable to tear my eyes away from her taut arms. Her muscles showed through her blouse, and I felt a flush creeping up my neck.

"Normally I eat healthy, but occasionally I like to indulge in food that actually tastes good. The smash burger is yummy, like a heart attack on a plate." Carly grinned, then her eyes met mine, faltered, and shifted back to the menu. Damn, this woman still took my breath away. Objectively speaking, I'd seen better looking girls than Carly, but they were usually on the poster of the latest blockbuster movie, not someone you'd meet in real life. She was like a Goddess, but it was her magnetic aura that drew me to her, and try as I might to resist, maybe I was being kinda silly about the whole thing? I mean, why not get to know her better, and if it led to something more…

"Carly, how've you been?" Two women appeared at the table, one was short with dark hair, and the other had long red hair and a nose ring.

"Great, no complaints. This is my, um, an old friend from high school who just moved back to town, Ashley. Ashley, meet two of my favorite people, Marcy and Cameron." Carly introduced us, and for a split second I worried that they would sit at the table, which felt stupid once I thought about it. Carly and I were just friends, having a friendly dinner, and that was it. No reason for me to fear they would intrude.

"Do you want to join us?" Carly asked, then glanced in my direction. I shrugged my shoulders and grinned, praying they wouldn't.

"We just finished an early dinner. The babysitter can't stay late, because it's a weeknight, so we need to get home early. Oh, and Marcy has an interview in the morning for a job. Otherwise, we'd love to join you both. It was nice meeting you, Ashley." Cameron said, then winked at Carly before the two of them turned on their heels and left.

"They're good people, and they used to rent from me. Actually, Cam and Marcy live in a house I sold them three blocks from here. You're gonna like living in downtown Raleigh, lots of cool people in the area." Carly flashed that blinding smile again. It made me forget where I was for a second, but then I remembered to keep the conversation going.

"I remember as a kid that downtown was so empty, filled with abandoned old buildings. It's amazing how they've turned things around. Most of these businesses and restaurants weren't here when I left town twenty years ago," I said.

"Well," Carly leaned back in her chair with a confident smirk. "You can thank me for a lot of that. I started my real estate business buying those old buildings and fixing them up. I always saw potential here and knew we could bring the downtown back. It's all about believing in yourself, making goals and doing whatever it takes to make it happen. You've done a pretty decent job of that yourself. What you told me about Harvard, and that shit that happened to you, most people would have folded, hightailed it and run away. You took the bull by the horns and made a career for yourself despite the odds. Shows you have guts and determination. I like that." Carly's grin flattened out, and I saw fire in her eyes.

My stomach flipped. How the hell could I resist her? Every time I saw my teenage crush it hit me physically, made me want to, I didn't know… relive the past? My love life over the years had been sporadic at best, and the last time I'd committed myself to someone, he left me at the altar for a younger woman.

"Carly, I sent you a text yesterday and never heard back." A young woman in her early twenties was suddenly behind Carly and placed her hands on her shoulders in a very familiar way. Whoever she was, the woman appeared like she'd walked off the pages of a fashion magazine. Carly stiffened and glanced up to see who it was. She blushed, then leaned forward, so the hands slipped off her.

"Um, I've been busy. Work and stuff, you know, the usual." Carly put her face in her palms for a brief second, then looked up at the woman again, a look of confusion on her face. The stranger finally noticed me and frowned.

"Is this who you're fucking now? Aren't you going to introduce us?" A hint of annoyance crossed the girl's pinched face. Carly reached across the table and took my hand in hers, folding my fingers into her palm.

"This is Ashley." She stated, and I wished the ground would open up and swallow me. It felt like the entire restaurant was a stage, and a spotlight shone over our table. I glanced around, wondering if every person there was focused on us. All I could think about was Carly's hand holding mine, possessively sending a message to this woman that I belonged to her, and to back off. Butterflies danced in my stomach. Then, a disturbing thought struck me. Was she only holding it to get rid of this obviously pissed-off girl?

"You can't even remember my name can you?" The woman turned to leave, then smirked in my direction. "Honey, Carly does this to all the girls. Don't think she won't do the same to you."

Her heels click-clacked across the dining room floor. When she got to the door she opened it and waved her manicured fingers in my direction, then she slammed it behind her.

So much time had passed, and I had to admit, that young woman might be a clue as to the type of person Carly really was. Her eyes were gazing intently into mine. Memories flooded back of how we used to hold hands in her beat-up car, or at the movies. I remembered feeling like a fish out of water as a teenager, and how Carly's touch would ground me, make me feel accepted and loved for who I was. She'd always been full of herself, but underneath her self-assuredness was a kind person who lived to make me smile.

"I'm sorry about…" Carly began, then we were interrupted.

"What can I get for you this evening?" A waitress dressed head to toe in black asked, startling me. I pulled my hand away from Carly's and snatched up the menu. Inwardly, I thanked the woman for saving me. This woman, who at one time was my reason for living, now scared the bejesus out of me.

———

"Thank you for dinner. Actually, I don't remember the food much, so I thank you for the company. I'm glad we're spending time together." Carly leaned against her car door, her eyes trapping mine. "I know we're just getting to know each other again…" She paused between every word, "…but you must know, you mean more to me than just friends. I've never forgotten you, Ashley." Carly laced her fingers around the back of my neck. Her scent, that vanilla and floral scent that turned me on so damn much flooded my nostrils. A warm flush traveled down my neck to my chest, and my nipples perked up at her touch.

"Carly, you don't know how much I want to believe you." I sighed, then pulled her in close, inhaling her fragrance as I did. My heart was thumping, but I couldn't figure out why. Was it fear, or lust? A combination of the two? Christ, I was probably overthinking the whole thing.

"I want you to—"

Carly's voice cut off mid-sentence, and it was my fault. I was kissing her. The taste of her lips against mine was so familiar, yet new. More powerful than my memories of Carly's youthful kisses, which drove me mad back then, and were doing so much more even now. The way she smelled and the texture of her soft skin around my lips felt so damn right. I was drowning in a heaven I'd never really forgotten, pushed back into my memories by her lips and arms wrapped around me. Every nerve ending in my body was singing as I melted into her embrace.

Carly pulled back and took my face in her hands. A soft sigh issued from her throat and then she crushed my mouth in another kiss. Carly tilted my head to the side and sucked on my tongue, then nibbled my bottom lip before it became a deep, passionate embrace that forced me to remember what her mouth felt like on other parts of my body. There was an urgency to it, as if we were making up for the time and distance that had kept us apart. Most importantly, it felt natural, like it was supposed to be just Carly and me holding each other up, the two of us against the world. It went on for what seemed like hours, but when it was over felt like mere seconds.

"Mmmm." Carly groaned, a heart-wrenching sound I remembered from years past, when we'd said goodbye.

Goodbye.

My God, what if she was just a player, hooking up with younger girls like that pissed-off woman at the table? What if he was like Frank, pretending to love me while fucking his surgical assistant?

Carly could destroy me.

"What...? Why are you pushing me away?" Carly pleaded as I pushed her back. Her mouth hung half open, and Carly's arms reached for me as I backed away. "Please, I'll do anything to..."

"I'm... I'm sorry Carly. I shouldn't have kissed you." I whispered, shaking my head slowly. Of all the things that would send me into a tailspin, it would be Carly, leaving me and breaking my heart. She had that power, and it would destroy me in a way that would make Frank's no-show at the altar seem like a minor blip in my timeline.

"I'm sorry." I stammered again, then I ran to my car. My hands trembled as I opened the door, my brain unable to catch up with my heart. Once I crashed into the seat, I attempted to slip the key into the ignition, but my hands were shaking too much. I took a few deep breaths, hoping to clear my head, then I looked out the window. Carly was leaning against her Jaguar, her back to the street, shoulders shaking. I'd only seen her cry once, and that was the night we were forced to say goodbye. We were reliving that night two decades later, and it was my fault. As teenagers I'd never seen her show even a hint of weakness, always in control of her every emotion. Carly's strength was what drew me to her, but the fact that she'd lost it whenever I was involved, only made me crave her more.

"What the hell have I done?" I groaned, then looked into the rear-view mirror, surprised to see black streaks sliding down my cheeks.

———

"I'm happy you found a new apartment, sweetie, though you don't look terribly excited." Aunt Dottie handed me a glass of chardonnay. She was my favorite relative, and I'd been grateful she'd taken me in while I found a place. We'd always had a strong bond, and though she was family, I truly thought of her as a best friend.

I wondered how much I could tell her about my evening. When I got to her house she'd immediately asked what was wrong. I'd shrugged it off, hoping to avoid any questions, but she'd always had a way of divining my moods, fishing out all the details I held back from everyone else.

"It's on Fayetteville Street downtown, that big apartment building with mirrored walls next to the Raleigh Savings And Trust building. I'm renting it from someone I knew in high school, Carly. We went to dinner after I signed the lease, and, well, things didn't go the way I thought they would." I sighed, not wanting to get into the particulars of the disastrous evening. The thing was, I needed to say something about it. I felt so uncomfortable, knowing I'd hurt her. Carly never cried. Don't ask me how I knew it, but I did.

"Carly? Do you mean that girl you were in love with in high school?" Aunt Dottie asked, a grin spreading across her rosy cheeks. I could tell she'd had more than one glass of wine. Normally, she wasn't this forthcoming.

"How...? How did you know? I never told you about Carly." I was flabbergasted.

"No dear, you never said a word about Carly. You didn't have to. But, I remember it like it was yesterday, that young woman always following you. Whenever you came over to visit, she was there, tagging along. You were always smiling, which beat the hell out of the brooding teenager you were before you met her. It reminded me of how I felt about your Uncle Gordon. I never wanted him out of my sight. Damn, I miss him to this day." Aunt Dottie's husband had died when I was young and she'd never remarried.

"So, why did you move back to Raleigh? Wasn't it to start afresh, to find new adventures? Because if there are any other reasons, you need to examine them. You should embrace life, not run away from it." She stated, locking her slightly blood-shot eyes to mine. As usual, she had a point.

"You know why I moved back to Raleigh." I waited for her to interject, and when she didn't, I continued. "Because of Frank, and his dumping me for another woman. Being left at the altar wasn't my finest moment. I'm not ready to be with anyone. It's too soon."

"But you weren't really in love with Frank, were you?" She held up her glass, as if toasting herself for accurately figuring it all out when I couldn't.

She was right, of course, but I didn't want to even contemplate the misery I'd feel if I started something with the first, and possibly only, person I'd ever loved. If Carly betrayed me like Frank had, it would destroy me. When Frank abandoned me at the altar, it changed the way I thought about the world. I now distrusted everyone, regardless of how well I knew them. Even if I never felt for Frank what I should have felt for a husband, the humiliation had never left me.

"No, I wasn't. That doesn't mean it didn't hurt though." I sighed. "I have to admit I felt a certain sense of, I don't know, relief? Part of me is glad that it didn't work out. The problem is, I messed things up tonight. It's just—" I started, but she interrupted me with questions I was too afraid to answer.

"Is Carly still in love with you?" She stared at me over her wine glass, an eyebrow lifted, then dropped the bomb.

"Are you still in love with her?"

CHAPTER

Six

CARLY

"HONEY, I have a meeting at the Garden Club, and then I'm getting fitted for the gown I'm wearing to the charity ball. Carly will take you to your doctor's appointment." Mom said. As usual, she was the only person capable of getting Dad to act like a somewhat reasonable person, though this morning the old man was putting up resistance.

"What the hell, Frances? I'm capable of driving myself. She needs to be closing the Blankenship deal." Dad glared at me. The breakfast room was painted bright yellow with red trim that Mom said was supposed to make everyone more cheerful in the morning. Feng shui? Whatever it was, its mystical powers were not working today.

"Grayson, if I let you drive yourself you won't go. You'll end up at some greasy spoon and make your ulcer worse." She glanced at her watch impatiently, then noticed Dad's scowl. "This is not a request. Carly will take you to the appointment, but Carter will pick you up. He wants to take you to lunch. Now put your jacket on and scoot." She pecked him on the cheek, grabbed her purse and hurried out.

Mom refused to call my brother Carter by his nickname, Inky, and blissfully ignored the head to toe tattoos covering him. Living in a world of her own, my mother ignored what she didn't like and pretended that our family was perfect, as if we lived in a TV sitcom from the 1950s. I think that was why her marriage to Dad worked. She ignored his foul moods, and pretended he was the star of Leave it to Beaver.

"Good. Your mother's gone. Now, this is what will really happen this morning."

"Shit." I groaned, then Dad carried on talking.

"You're going to take me to…" he grumbled, but was interrupted by Mom, who was standing at the door.

"Carly Elizabeth Poindexter, I'm going to wash your mouth out with soap! You know how much I hate the brown word. Grayson, if you bully Carly into letting you cancel that appointment, you will regret it. Trust me on this. Now, get in her car and go. I have too much to do to be babysitting you today." She kissed Dad on the cheek again, then pecked mine for good measure. "Don't let him get away with his usual nonsense. Oh, and watch your language." She wagged her finger at me, then left.

"You heard her, Dad, let's get this over with." I sighed, not in the mood to deal with his tantrums today. Usually I'd let the verbal abuse slide, knowing when to pick my battles, but since my disastrous night with Ashley, I rivaled Dad for the title of Grumpiest Person in Raleigh.

"Fine, I'll go." Dad snatched his jacket off the back of his chair and stomped out. I took a few deep breaths and followed behind, hoping Dad would keep his mouth shut for the ride, but knowing he wouldn't.

———

"I know I keep harping on about this, but the Blankenship deal is very important to me and the firm. We stand to make a great deal of cash if we can get that hippy to sell those apartments." Dad uttered, then swiped at his forehead with the back of his hand. I noticed something I'd never seen before, or perhaps didn't want to notice. Fear. He was afraid, and maybe it was his mortality that had him on edge instead of his usual bad temper.

"Dad, I am heading over to the Millbrook Arms Apartments to speak with Mr. Turner. If he refuses to budge, I'll offer him an additional ten percent, as long as Mr. Blankenship approves it." I said. We were waiting for his appointment with the internist at UNC Rex Medical Center.

"Don't worry about Seth Blankenship. He'll pony up any amount of money to buy that dump. Never forget that Seth has been a loyal client since I opened the business almost forty years ago. Whatever he wants, he gets. Now, get the hell out of here, oh, and call your brother and tell him to come a few minutes early." Dad's paperwork lay in his lap untouched.

"If you don't fill that out, it's going to take you longer, Dad." I stood, ready to bolt if he tried to start something. He glared at me, then smiled. It was scary, since he did it so rarely.

"Sorry I'm such a pain in the ass, but I really hate doctors. Thanks for being here. Now, get out." Dad picked up his pen and started filling out the forms. I stood stock still, my mouth hanging open. It was the nicest thing he'd said to me in years. "I said go." Dad mumbled, then elbowed me in the knee.

"Yes, sir."

———

Mom had asked me to take Dad to his appointment yesterday. Normally, I would have tried getting out of it, but I had an ulterior motive. The appointment was in an office building next to the hospital, and I wanted to speak with Ashley about the kiss.

I'd barely slept the night before, tossing and turning, my brain refusing to turn off. When I finally fell asleep, I relived that moment over and over in my dreams. Ashley had kissed me, and she was the one who started it. It was she who fell into my arms and temporarily made real what I'd dreamed about for years. What I didn't get was why she'd run away.

Seeking Ashley out at work was risky, and skirted the border of stalking, but I needed answers. Intruding on her life was not what I wanted to do, but I needed to know how she actually felt. Ashley would never have put her arms around me the way she did last night if the feeling was not mutual. That kiss felt real, and the way her body responded to mine felt real. But, if Ashley had decided she wanted nothing to do with me, I'd respect that. I might not like it, but I'd back off.

My pulse throbbed in my ear as I walked through the entrance of the ER. A small crowd was in the waiting area, so I stood behind them, hoping to pull myself together unobserved. I wasn't used to this feeling, the uneasiness of vulnerability I'd fought so hard to defeat since I'd left the Marines. Women flocked to me, chased me in fact, and it was scary to find I was now doing the same to Ashley.

A male nurse with bright red hair I remembered from Dad's visit to the ER was working at the main desk. It took all of my self-control not to run out of the ER, to brave the few steps I had to walk to that desk. But, if I didn't force one foot in front of the other, I'd never know if I had a chance with Ashley or not. I took a deep breath and moved forward.

"Excuse me, you don't happen to know if Ashley James is available?"

The nurse said nothing for a moment, looking me up and down with suspicion.

"Who wants to know?"

I thought people only said that in movies. My heart galloped in my chest, and I felt my throat closing up. Please, don't give me any problems, dude. I'm not here to hurt Ashley, only to get answers. I glanced at his name tag and addressed him properly.

"Mark, my name is Carly Poindexter. Would you please tell her I am here, and that I'd like a word with her."

He pursed his lips and studied me for a few more uncomfortable seconds. Finally, he responded. "Just a moment. I'll see if she's able to speak with you." The man strolled away, turning his head around a couple of times, as if to make sure I wasn't following him. Jesus, did I look crazed or something?

After what seemed like forever, Ashley strolled into the reception area. Our eyes locked, and she stopped in her tracks. I could feel myself flushing and noticed a similar look on Ashley's face. She whispered something to the other nurse, laid a clipboard on the counter, and stepped forward.

"Let's go outside for a moment. I can't talk for long." Ashley muttered, then kept walking toward the entrance. I followed behind as casually as I could. Feeling like I was being watched, I turned my head back for a moment to see that nurse, Mark, observing us with narrowed eyes as we exited the building. Outside on the sidewalk, people milled around us, and I realized she'd done this for a reason, so we wouldn't be alone. She led me to a bus stop with a bench and we both sat, Ashley taking pains to keep a few inches of space between us. She looked over my shoulder, up to the overcast sky, anywhere but into my eyes. My hands itched to touch her, to pull her into my chest, and to kiss her with the passion I knew she felt too. A long moment passed, and at last the words I needed to say spilled out.

"Ashley, about the other night. I'm confused. You're the one who kissed me, and you have to understand I—"

"That was a mistake, Carly. It's my fault, and I assume full responsibility for it." Her emerald green eyes finally met mine, and they were glassy and wet. Ashley's discomfort was obvious, but she also needed to know my heart was breaking. I reached over, intending to take her hand, but she crossed her arms over her chest. My hand landed back in my lap with a thud.

"Ashley, I know you're feeling this too. The chemistry between us is real. I don't understand why you're denying it. Please, give me one more chance, give us one more chance. Let me take you to a movie, or a walk in the park. Let me just be with you." I pleaded in a whisper.

Ashley looked up to the sky, and her mouth angled down into a frown. Her hand reached toward mine, but she pulled it back, shook her head, and got to her feet.

"Look, Carly, it's just too soon. As you know I recently got dumped, left at the altar in front of hundreds of wedding guests. I only moved back to town two weeks ago, and dating is off the table. Being hurt again is something I'm not setting myself up for. If you'll excuse me, I need to get back to work. I'm very sorry, but I just can't do this right now." Ashley walked away. I stared after her, hoping she'd look back, but she never did.

———

At a stoplight on Capitol Boulevard I punched the steering wheel.

"Damn it, Ashley, why are you doing this?" I yelled, provoking a look from the driver beside me. I rolled up the window, sank in my seat and stared straight ahead. When the light turned green, I hit the gas and raced forward to get away from the pack of cars around me.

"I'm done. No more love. I've had a good life avoiding it. Drama is kept to a minimum, and I'm able to focus on my work and make great money. Commitment is for mental patients, not for me." My words were hollow though, and I knew it.

Moments later the Millbrook Arms Apartments came into view, and I turned into the pothole-ridden parking lot. Glancing around at the buildings, I wondered why Mr. Turner was resisting our offer. They were barely up to code, and couldn't be making him much money. The offer Seth Blankenship was making would set Turner up for the rest of his life. The North Raleigh area was being rebuilt with trendy shops and restaurants. Underneath the decrepit apartment buildings was land worth far more than he paid for.

"Mr. Turner, please let Seth Blankenship write you a check, because I don't want to deal with my Dad kicking my ass if you don't." I muttered to myself, then picked up the folder on the passenger seat. Dread filled me as I stepped out of the car and headed toward the rental office. Nothing was going my way today, and I had a feeling this meeting wouldn't end with Turner signing a contract.

Inside the folder was an offer ten per cent higher than the last one. I was only allowed to show it to him if he balked at the original price again. I rang the bell, and after a few moments the door opened. Turner glared at me and started to shut it.

"Please, Mr. Turner. I need to speak with you." Good God, it was like every person I'd seen today was determined to give me a rough time.

"Miss Poindexter. I'm sorry, it's just you know what my answer will be." He waited for me to speak, and when I said nothing, he continued. "It's still no. I wish you'd stop bothering me with these offers, because it's useless." He said, then with a shake of his head he stepped aside, and ushered me into his office.

Turner was a throwback to the seventies, and peace signs and dust ruled his domain. He was solidly built, and his graying hair fell past his shoulders. A poster of John Lennon hung on the wall behind his desk, and I swore I could smell weed. He gestured toward the chair in front of his desk. After I sat, I leaned forward and placed the folder in front of him. He opened, then shut it with a look of disgust. Fuck me, what a waste of time.

"I've been authorized by Seth Blankenship to make you a new offer. It's ten per cent higher than the previous one." I muttered, my usual determination gone. All I could see in my mind was Ashley's face telling me to give up, to leave her alone. I had no energy left to talk this man into giving me a bong hit, much less selling us his property. Glancing out the side window, I saw a playground with kids playing on it, their mothers sitting on a dilapidated bench watching them. The swings and sliding board were old, built on a concrete slab. Half of the swings were missing seats, and weeds sprouted through cracks in the pavement. Why he wanted to hold on to this eyesore was beyond me.

"Do you want to know why I'm turning this down?" Turner's thin voice cut through the air. I turned back to him and nodded. He pushed the folder to my side of the desk.

"I bought this complex when the neighborhood hit bottom, when gunshots and sirens were heard on a daily basis. It cost next to nothing, and this current offer you're making..." He pointed at the folder, "...is almost twenty times what I paid for it. You probably think I'm a fool for turning you down."

"It has crossed my mind, sir." I murmured, shrugging my shoulders.

"Just now I saw you looking at those kids outside on the

playground. Their parents struggle to find affordable housing, especially now that developers like yourself are pricing them out of the neighborhoods they've spent their entire lives in. Where are those kids to go? What about the real people who can't afford to pay the astronomical rents you want to charge them?" His thin lips pressed together, expecting me to put up an argument. I had none to give.

"I'm sorry to have bothered you Mr. Turner. Have a good day."

I had no fight left in me, so I gave him a half-smile, picked up the folder and strolled back to my truck. Before I hopped in the front seat I looked around, the peeling paint and drooping clotheslines next to the buildings standing in stark contrast to the new loft apartments sprouting up all over the neighborhood. But I could hear the sounds of happy children coming from the playground on the other side of the building. The argument Turner made was compelling, and I actually admired him for sticking to his guns.

Dad would make my life miserable, but I'd recommend to Mr. Blankenship that he look for another property. There were other rundown buildings in the area he could bulldoze. Hopefully he'd leave Mr. Turner and the residents who lived here in peace.

CHAPTER
Seven

ASHLEY

"ARE YOU THE NEW TENANT? I saw movers bringing stuff in this morning, and I've never seen you around before. Oh, my name is Inky." A stunning man with dark hair covered in tattoos held his hand out for me to shake. I put my basket of laundry down and shook it.

"It's a pleasure to meet you. My name is Ashley, and yes, I'm the new tenant." The guy was friendly, which added to my good feelings about the move. I loved my new apartment, and if I could make a friend or two in the building, so much the better.

"Moving is a pain in the ass. Are you new to the area?" He tossed detergent in the washer and stuffed his clothes inside.

"Yes, and no. I'm from here, but I've been gone for almost twenty years now. Just moved back. Raleigh has changed an awful lot since I've been gone. You don't happen to know of a place to find antiques, or vintage furniture? I only brought my bedroom with me, and I don't want the usual boring stuff you find at chain furniture stores." It broke my heart to give up so much of my furniture in the move, but I was determined to start over from scratch. A fresh start in every way, not just where I lived.

"I like you more just hearing that. No boring furniture, or anything at all for that matter. Yes, I know a lot of places to discover cool stuff. Maybe we can go shopping together. Actually, I have a better idea," Inky leaned over and turned the washer on.

"Put your clothes in the washer and you can come up to my place. We can have a glass of wine, and I can show off my furniture. I'd like to think I have funky taste. Oh, and I'll give you the lay of the land, tell you which of our neighbors to avoid, that sort of thing." His smile was infectious, and I grinned in response. What the hell, it could be fun. I could also use a new friend.

"This is home. Sorry it's a mess, but I'm allergic to cleaning. Well, except for the kitchen and bathroom. I'm not completely gross." My new neighbor let us into his apartment, and I was in love with the way he'd decorated. It suited him to a T. Unique artwork hung on the walls, brightly colored paintings that matched the tattoos covering his skin. Inky was right about the clutter. There was barely an empty spot on the tables, most of them filled with miniature Asian sculptures and bonsai plants. What struck me was how homey it felt, very comfortable and lived in.

"Have a seat and I'll pour us a glass. Merlot okay?"

I nodded and sat on a dusky purple velvet couch. Moments later Inky sat next to me and lifted his glass.

"A toast; to new neighbors and friends." His smile was so

huge and warm, and oddly familiar. I wondered for a moment if we'd met before, maybe as children?

"Okay, now let's talk about the lay of the land. Most of the peeps living here have been around a long time. They're a friendly bunch, and we have little get-togethers regularly. There are a couple of them you need to watch out for. On the first floor next to the entrance is an elderly man, Mr. Crandall. He's grumpy, but harmless. We all keep an eye out for him since he lives alone. Which apartment did you get?" His words came out in a gush, and it took a moment for me to remember my unit number.

"I'm on the sixth floor, 603."

"You took Grace's old place. I'm proud to say my match-making abilities hit solid gold with her. I introduced Grace to her husband, Michael. So you have me to thank for your new apartment." Inky sipped his wine, then put an index finger on his chin, and asked the question I dreaded most.

"Are you single? Or seeing someone special?" He cocked his head to the side and waited for my answer.

"Yes, and no. But, I'm recently out of a relationship, so I'm kinda keeping to myself if you know what I mean." I took a big gulp of my wine, hoping my answer would keep him from wanting to set me up with somebody. Plus, and I knew it was crazy, but I was hoping to hear from Carly. I'd told her to leave me alone, but a small part of me regretted that decision. Sleepless nights had been filled with images of her, and every time my phone buzzed, I'd hold my breath hoping she'd contacted me, despite me telling her not to.

"That's too bad, because there's a bartender at work who is relentlessly single, hot, and I'd love to see him with someone steady. His name is Mark. Oh, you must come to my bar. It's called Inky's, and it's only a few blocks away. Your first drink will be my treat!" He grinned.

"I will, as long as you don't try to set me up with Mark." I laughed. Inky faked a frown and then giggled.

"Sorry, I can't help it. I feel like the world is a gray place, so I'm always setting up my friends, adding color to their lives, know what I mean?" Inky sipped his drink, then continued the interrogation. "So where did you move here from?" He asked. I could tell it would be easy to open up to him, but I didn't want to give Inky my life story yet.

"Boston. I got a job at UNC Rex Hospital and decided to make a fresh start here in my hometown. It's been great being back, for the most part. Actually, I had an ex-girlfriend hit me up already." I said, then mentally kicked myself for saying too much. What if this man was weird about me liking both men and women? Inky's face lit up, and inwardly I sighed with relief.

"Really? That's fast. Are you going to go out with her?" He stood up and darted to the kitchen without waiting for my reply. When Inky returned, he had the wine bottle with him. Inky poured himself another glass and topped mine off. I mulled my words over, then gave in to the need to tell someone about how I really felt.

"Let's just say it's the wrong time. I'm still attracted to her, and the chemistry is like, wow, off the charts. But I need to spend some time on my own. All I'm interested in now is settling in and finding my groove here. If it was just a simple fling, or a friends with benefits situation, I'd be all for it. There's just too much history between us though, so I don't see it being simple, or a fling. She wants more, and I'm not in the right headspace for anything serious." I said, formulating in words what I'd been thinking since I'd told Carly I didn't want to see her anymore. "I can tell you're a bartender, because I'm telling you stuff I've not even said aloud to myself." I raised my glass to Inky, and he laughed. Then his eyes widened, and he grabbed my hand.

"Hey, I've got a fabulous idea. You wanna play dress up and crash a party? And when I say dress up, I mean wear something special, like an evening gown. It's this Saturday, and it's probably going to be a little boring, but the food will be excellent, and it's free booze. You can be my plus one! Please? I don't want to go alone. My sister is throwing it, mostly to impress her clients. I'll wear this cool tuxedo I got at a vintage clothing shop a couple of blocks from here. Let me show it to you." Inky raced out of the room and returned with a stunning vintage tuxedo that appeared in perfect condition. I thought about it for less than a second.

"Yes, I would love to go to this party."

———

Work kept me busy all week, which helped since it bummed me out that Carly never texted or called. I guessed my words got through to her, and she would respect my wishes after all. I told her it was bad timing, that I didn't want us to rekindle what was a teenage romance, but… damn, I still kind of hoped she'd try. In theory, I was relieved. Realistically, part of me regretted telling Carly to back off. Whatever, I was the one who decided not to pursue it. My heart was still healing from my last relationship, and I didn't need the pressure of a new one. Life was too short for regrets, and I didn't need a romantic partner to make me feel complete.

Seven o'clock rolled around, and I had promised Inky I'd meet him at eight. Time to pull out the fancy gown I kept in the back of the closet wrapped in plastic. It was what I was supposed to have worn to my wedding reception on the beach, and I'd spent a small fortune on it. As I pulled it out, I felt my throat closing up and pressure building behind my eyes. I knew I hadn't been in love with Frank, but that didn't mean the pain wasn't real. I'd not looked at the gown since my tragic wedding day, and as I pulled the delicate fabric out of the bag, a wave of despair rolled through me. Sitting on the side of the bed, I held the gown to my chest and struggled not to cry. I realized I was crushing it, so I laid it next to me, then fell back on the mattress and curled up on my side.

"What if it had been someone I really cared for who stood me up? I wasn't even in love with Frank and I'm still in mourning for our relationship. What if it had been Carly who abandoned me at the altar?" I whispered. A tear dropped from my cheek to the mattress. I stood up and headed to the bathroom to splash cold water on my face.

"Stop caring about this. It was for the best. Frank not showing up proves how little you can trust people. He didn't care about me enough to tell me he didn't want to go through with the marriage, humiliating me in front of everyone we knew. If we hadn't worked at the same hospital, I'd probably still be in Boston, happily getting on with my life." I stated to my reflection in the mirror. "Just stop caring and give yourself a little TLC for a change."

Of course, the bitch of the matter was, I did care about love. If I didn't care, I wouldn't have given Carly a second thought, and I wouldn't be so torn up inside at the thought of never hearing from her again. How could I not care for her? The night we parted was burned in my memory, and the attraction hadn't gone away. If anything it had grown. When I went to Harvard, and even beyond school, I went on a string of first dates, always turning the second date down, because they just couldn't compare to her. But did I want to set myself up for rejection again? I answered aloud, to the judgemental eyes gazing at me from the mirror.

"Hell no. Life's too short to willingly set yourself up for pain. Now let's put on some makeup and have a good time. Inky's your date for the evening, and we will have a blast."

————

"Wow, you look stunning." Inky surprised me with a hug, then stood back from his door. "What do you think?" He asked, then spun around. His raven-black hair had been meticulously gelled back, shiny like a silent movie star. The tuxedo had a tail-coat, and I'd never seen a tie quite like the one he wore around his neck.

"You look drop-dead gorgeous, Inky, like you walked out of the Great Gatsby. Seriously, I'm not just saying that." I stood back and admired him.

"Well, I do have a confession to make. We might be a little overdressed, but my sister's work parties can sometimes be a little dull. I want to liven it up a bit. You'll like her. She's also single and very attractive, or at least that's what all her girl-friend's say." He winked, then turned and shut the door.

"You know my answer to that. I'm not dating anyone." I laughed. Inky grabbed my hand and dragged me to the eleva-tor. When we got in, he surprised me.

"Why are you hitting the button for the penthouse? I thought we were going out?" I asked as the elevator doors closed behind us.

"My sister lives there. The reason I go to her boring parties is I can drink and have fun, and not have to worry about driving home. Feel free to imbibe as much booze as you can safely hold, and eat all you want. Getting home is a breeze, and you won't break any laws either."

Moments later the elevator opened. Inky took my hand and led me to the solitary door in the tiny hallway.

"It's probably not as boring as I let on. She always invites potential clients though, and warns me to be on my best behavior. I'm usually good for the first half of the evening. For the second half, anything goes." Inky winked and opened the door.

Bossa Nova music filled the space, and several couples were already on the improvised dance floor, which I assumed was the living room, but most of the furniture was gone. Our hostess also had a substantial art collection, but hers was more elegant and refined than her brother's. Subdued paintings filled the walls, which were painted a muted heather with soft track lighting giving the room a subtle glow. Inky's sister had great taste, and I could see why the room was already full, despite it being relatively early.

"You were right, we are a tad overdressed." I murmured, and Inky cackled.

"All eyes will be on us, and we'll be the hit of the party. I hope you can dance. My parents are very conservative, sent me to cotillion to learn how to dance and be a proper southern gentleman. I might not be proper, but I am the king of the tango, so I expect you to dance your ass off." Inky grabbed two glasses of champagne off a waiter's tray, and handed me one.

The champagne was superb, which surprised me. Most functions like this served the cheap stuff. I snuck a glance at Inky, envious of his perpetual smile. It had been so long since I'd cut loose and had fun. Tonight I would forget about my problems and really live, have a good time. Instead of taking another small sip of the bubbly, I downed my glass.

"Atta girl!" Inky smacked me on the shoulder. "I like your style, Ashley. But before we get carried away, let's grab some hors d'oeuvres. Don't want to get too drunk, too fast." He looped his arm through mine and dragged me to a table laden with goodies. Inky picked up two small plates and handed me one, and then I heard a velvety voice drawl from behind us.

"Inky. You look rakish as always. Who are you with?"

I put my plate down because my hands were trembling, the nerve endings in my skin coming alive at the sound of her. I turned slowly around and confronted the devilish woman that had haunted my thoughts since I'd run away from her. A confident smile spread across her face when our eyes met.

"Hello, Carly."

"SO, you've met my brother, Inky?"

It stunned me to see Ashley with him. Knowing she was downstairs on the sixth floor was challenging, and I debated nightly if I should knock on her door or not. So far, I'd stood in front of it twice, wondering how Ashley would react if she opened the door to see me with a smile and a hand over my heart. Common sense had prevailed. Knowing my bed was above hers, and that I could be on her doorstep in less than two minutes, made every second I spent alone even more torturous. Looking at her now, it took every ounce of self-control not to kick everyone out and drag her to my bedroom.

Ashley was downright elegant, like she was attending a high-society function. Her normally wavy strawberry-blonde hair was straightened and hanging past her bare, milky white shoulders. Her scarlet gown clung to her curves, and the only jewelry she wore was a simple gold chain with a solitary emerald hanging between her ample cleavage.

Everyone in the room had noticed Ashley and Inky's entrance. My eyes traveled up her body, inch by inch until our eyes met. Ashley's wide-eyed look of wonder confirmed my suspicions. She didn't know Inky was my younger brother. I might not be superstitious, or really religious, but I was starting to believe in fate. How else could she be here?

Ashley turned to Inky and stared hard at him, then swiveled in my direction.

"Now it makes sense why you looked familiar." Ashley avoided my eyes. "Inky and I met in the laundry room and hit it off. You know, I'd wondered if we'd met as kids or something, though I'm bewildered that we've not met before." Ashley drank a healthy gulp of her cocktail.

"You two know each other? It's a small world, isn't it?" My brother said, then got a look in his eye that terrified me.

"Inky, we went to high school together. I've told you about her before. Ashley James? We were, um, very close in our senior year. Remember?" I winked. I didn't want to put Ashley on the spot by going into the details of our prior relationship. She'd already made it clear she wanted nothing from me, and even though I felt heat between my legs just being in the same room with her, I'd do my best to respect that. If she only wanted a casual friendship, so be it. Ashley would be mine again, but she would come to me when she was good and ready.

"You're Ashley? How the hell didn't I... well, it's nice to meet you after all these years. I heard an awful lot about you." Inky's grin grew wider, and I could see the wheels spinning in his head. I would have to take him aside and tell him to lay off the matchmaking. He'd never tried it before with me, because he knew I wasn't into relationships. Now Inky could see an opening, a way to work his meddlesome magic.

"If you guys are brother and sister, how come we never met? I used to spend a lot of time with Carly when we were teenagers." Ashley wondered. Inky placed his drink on a table and took a step back.

"Mom shipped me off to fancy-ass Saint Christopher's School in Virginia to make a gentleman out of me. It's a stuffy boys boarding school, and I'm still recovering from the scars it left on my soul. As you can see..." Inky spun around and threw his arms in the air, "...it utterly failed!"

The three of us burst into laughter, and I was so grateful for my brother's ability to put anyone at ease. When I'd first noticed the two of them walk through the door, my heart had skipped a beat, and I deliberately held back, waiting for them to get drinks before coming forward. I didn't want to look too anxious, or desperate. Though, the way my heart was beating now, I wondered if that was how bad it had gotten. Shit, desperation wasn't a good look on anyone.

"So how did you get the penthouse? I mean, I know your Dad's real-estate firm owns the place, but I had no idea you lived here. Why didn't you tell me you lived in this building?" A suspicious look settled on Ashley's face, replacing the easy grin from just a moment ago. Shit, she was going there.

"Dad doesn't own this building. Carly does." Inky said, then snatched Ashley's empty glass from her hand, and strolled to the bar to get them refilled. Ashley crossed her arms over her chest, eyes narrowed.

"When I signed the lease, it said Poindexter Realty." Ashley stated, and I cringed.

"That's the name of my company. Dad's business is Raleigh Real Estate & Development. We share an office, you know, work together, though he forgets that most of the time." I sighed, seeing this battle was probably lost, and yet another load of bullshit would come between us. She'd think horrible things about me, and I'd have to change her mind. Again.

Ashley glanced away, a shadow passing over her face. When she looked back, my shoulders stiffened, knowing whatever she had to say would not be good.

"Wait, a minute. The rent you're charging is half of what I paid in Boston. I realize this is a smaller city, but it makes little sense that I got such a good deal. You aren't expecting some kind of quid pro quo arrangement? Expecting me to sleep with you in exchange for paying lower rent? Because if you are you'll be…"

"Here you go, Ashley." Inky handed her a drink. "Oh look, some of my employees are here. Since you're new in town, they'll be excellent friends to have. Let me introduce you." He looped his arm through Ashley's, but she shrugged it off.

"Inky, if you don't mind, I need to have a word with Carly. Alone." She glared at me. Inky gave me the side eye, then her. "Yeah… I'll talk to you both in a little while." He hightailed it to the other side of the room, a look of confusion on his face.

Damn, she was going to let me have it. The question was, did I want it to be in public, or could I drag her somewhere in private, so she wouldn't give me grief in front of my guests. My eyes darted around the room, then I saw that the balcony was empty.

"Ashley, let's take this outside." I grasped her elbow, intending to lead her forward, but she shook it off. Ashley stretched her arm out, indicating I should go first and she'd follow.

Fine. Be that way.

The balcony stretched the length of the building, so I took her to the furthest corner away from the sliding glass doors. My heart galloped in my chest, afraid she was going to either cuss me out or slug me. If this was anybody else, I would've laughed it off and sent them packing, but this was Ashley, and I could see why she might think I was doing something shady. Thing was, I wasn't. Maybe I could change the subject? Get her to focus on something else, anything but me and what she was accusing me of.

I leaned against the railing and glanced up. There was a full moon, and even the stars looked brighter than usual. I turned to see Ashley's face in her hands, and she was shaking her head. Without thinking, I put my arm around her and drew her closer. Removing her hands from her face, she glared in my direction.

"Carly, please say you're charging me the same rent as everyone else. Please, tell me this entire arrangement, me signing that lease wasn't a way to get in my pants. I remember that woman from the restaurant, angry that you couldn't even remember her name. I'm not lining up to be another one of your conquests."

I pressed my lips together, not used to being questioned about my ethics. Honestly, it was pissing me off.

"Ashley, you are paying the same rent as everyone else. Go ask anyone in there, well, except my brother. Inky gets the family discount." I bit my tongue, not wanting to say anything to make things worse.

"Yeah, right. You won't expect any type of special compensation from me? Because if you are, you can forget about it." Ashley bit her words off and started to stalk off. I grabbed her shoulder and spun her around.

"What the hell? Why do you think I'd pull one over on you? I don't need to pull tricks to get women in bed, and the fact you think I would speaks volumes for how you really feel about me. Shit, that woman at Beasley's restaurant? Damn right, I didn't remember her name. You know why? Because I didn't give two shits about her." I crossed my arms over my chest, and realized how callous that made me sound. "That woman knew all along that I wanted nothing serious. I made it perfectly clear from the very start."

Ashley placed her hands on her hips and glared at me with her brilliant green eyes.

"I care about you, not some silly girl who apparently couldn't understand that I wanted nothing more than a one-night stand." I took a deep breath, trying to keep my temper in check. "You know, maybe you're right. This isn't the time for us. Maybe it's just some fucked-up fantasy in my head that you and I could still have something, that our connection never went away." No one, not even Ashley James would get away with accusing me of this underhanded shit. "Now if you'll excuse me, I have guests to attend to. Enjoy the party."

———

"I don't know what went down with you two, but Ashley looks miserable. I tried to get her to talk, but she clams up and says nothing's wrong." Inky whispered in my ear. I glanced over at her standing in a corner nursing her drink. I'd kept my eyes on her all night, noticing that wherever I went, she was always a few feet away. Not talking, just staring at me as I talked to clients and friends.

"Ashley had the nerve to accuse me of giving her cheap rent so I could get in her pants. You know me, Inky. I don't have to resort to stupid tactics like that to get anyone in bed." I turned away from Ashley, hoping she didn't see the anger boiling inside me.

"Shit. Do you want me to say something to her?" Inky asked, then glanced in her direction. Ashley looked away, and I knew she could see we were talking about her. I was about to beg my brother not to say anything, when Ashley pushed herself off the wall and sauntered over.

"Can I have a word with you Carly?" She asked, and I noticed her words were slurred, just the tiniest bit. I glanced down at her hand, noticing she'd switched from champagne to something more potent. Her green eyes were wet, and I felt my knees growing weak. I couldn't resist her, never could. Ashley could ask me for anything and I'd give it to her.

"Excuse us." I nodded to Inky, then led her back to the balcony. Another couple was in our old spot, so I walked us to the other side which faced the busy streets of downtown.

Ashley leaned against the railing. I joined her, careful to stand a few inches away. She was staring at the traffic down below, then she turned and faced me, her skin paler than usual.

"I'm sorry. I shouldn't have accused you of what I did. I, well, I was being a brat. You didn't deserve it." Ashley murmured, staring down at her feet. I reached out and placed my hand on her shoulder, rewarded by a small smile crossing her face as she stared into my eyes.

"Apology accepted. Though, for the record I'll never, ever resort to dirty tricks like that. If you want to be left alone, I'll respect your wishes." I wanted to pull her into my arms, touch her, feel her warmth underneath the palms of my hands, but I resisted the urge. No way was I going to scare her off now. Ashley turned back toward the railing, then looked up.

"Do you see the stars above us? They're beautiful." When she pointed up a cloud passed over. "Damn it, the moon is gone now." Her voice trailed off, and she moved an inch closer. My arm itched to wrap around her, to pull Ashley tight against me. I wanted to touch her so damn bad. Instead, I hoped my words could bring her to me, willingly, not coerced.

"Look down at the street, at the cars below us. All the flashing, sparkling lights you'd ever want. I often stand out here alone to think, you know, to clear my head. Something about the stars overhead and the cars driving below makes me feel like nothing can touch me. Like nothing can touch us." I whispered. Ashley's smile widened, then she looked down like it embarrassed her. Fuck me, she didn't need to feel ashamed of anything around me. It was as if she was afraid of her feelings, afraid, shit, that I'd hurt her.

How could I breach this wall she'd erected between us?

"Just because you aren't pulling something shady on me to get in my pants, it doesn't mean you will have your way with me. I know you Carly Poindexter. In high school you had everyone wrapped around your finger, always getting anything you wanted." Ashley said, biting her lower lip. Damn, I wanted to do that for her, nibble on her full red lips, then cover her mouth with mine. But first, I had to make her want it. I took Ashley's hand and pulled her inside.

"Where are you taking me?" She asked as I led her through the sea of couples dancing. I turned and stood before her. We stared into each other's eyes for what seemed like forever, and then I crushed her into my chest.

"Let's dance, baby. We never got the chance to do this when we were teenagers." I smiled, though I knew she would push back. Call it intuition, but I sensed her need, her desire to be touched. I could feel she wanted it. Ashley pressed her breasts against mine, and I could feel her heartbeat hammering inside of her.

"You are the most beautiful woman in this room." I whispered, then gently kissed the tender flesh beneath her ear. She fell slightly forward and wrapped her arms tightly around my waist. A soft moan escaped from her throat.

Mission accomplished.

"You are so sure of yourself, thinking you can do whatever you want. Jesus, Carly, what's gotten into you?" Ashley said, but the entire time she was bitching, she was also melting into my arms, moving her feet in response to mine, rubbing her body against me. I placed my index finger under her chin, and lifted it so her lips were inches away.

"You've always been such a romantic." Ashley whispered. I

chuckled, knowing she was the only person ever to accuse me of that.

"Ashley," My lips glanced off the side of her neck, and then I whispered in her ear, "You are the one woman in my life who's ever said that, much less thought it. You know why?" She shook her head, locking those intense emerald-green eyes to mine. "Because you're the reason. I've only ever been romantic with you."

———

A fight broke out between two tenants who lived next to each other, both complaining about the other being noisy. Putting them in the same room with booze had not been the brightest idea I'd ever had, so I left Ashley to break it up. When I returned, she was dancing with Inky, and the crowd was thinning out. I was about to cut in when I felt a tap on my shoulder.

"Have you seen our host, Carly Poindexter?" Cameron, my former tenant asked me, a curious look on his face.

Smartass.

"What on earth are you talking about?" I blushed, knowing exactly what he was talking about.

"Well, my friend Carly doesn't believe in relationships, only in casual sex. No commitments for her. Doesn't want to be tied down, a no-strings-attached kind of girl. I was talking to her brother who tells me that she's mooning over someone." He scanned the crowd, then pointed toward Ashley. "That girl. She's the one making Carly insane."

"I don't want to talk about it."

Cam said nothing. He didn't have to. The shit-eating grin on his face forced me to respond.

"Fine. Just don't spread it around. I got a reputation, know what I mean?" I shrugged my shoulders, then poked him in the chest. "You promise not to run around town with this?" I asked. Cam rolled his eyes, then nodded. I gave him the quick version of my relationship with Ashley.

"So, you're telling me that this is your high-school sweetheart you've never gotten over? Like for twenty years? Damn, you've got it bad." Cam laughed, and I felt a flush creeping up my neck.

"Who the hell are you to talk? You and Marcy are..." I began, then a couple of guests interrupted us to say their goodbyes. Marcy sidled up to me while I was giving them my thanks for coming and sang in my ear.

"Ashley and Carly sitting in a tree..."

"Fuck. You. Marcy." I said through gritted teeth as the couple took off. She jumped away, afraid I really meant it. I opened my arms.

"I'm just messing with you, Marcy," I laughed. She wrapped her arms around my waist and kissed me on the cheek, then she let go of me, and threw her arms around her husband.

"We'd better go before Carly really gets mad." She said to Cam, who threw up his hands in mock fear.

"Too late." Cam glanced at his watch. "Yeah, looks like the party's winding down. I need to make sure the sitter gets home in time. Let's get together soon, you know, the four of us." He winked.

"Get out, both of you!" I laughed, then hustled them to the door. Shit, I didn't want my friends speculating about something I was unsure of. Ashley might be responding to me now, but that could change on a dime. Moments later, all thoughts of Ashley turning me away flew out the window, as she stumbled over to me and whispered in my ear.

"Do you want me to stay with you tonight?"

Nine

CARLY

"YOUR PARTY WAS FABULOUS, though I must admit I think it was the company. Usually they're a big snooze fest." Inky teased, swaying just the teensiest bit.

Only the three of us remained; my brother, me, and Ashley. We were on the balcony, enjoying the nighttime sky and the chill breeze coming in off the river. I was torn between telling Inky to hightail it out of there, and keeping him as a buffer between Ashley and me. Tension had been building since she asked to stay the night. If I was smart, I'd get my brother to take Ashley home, but I'd never been smart when it came to this woman. Moments later, my dilemma was solved when Inky did something, well, Inky-like.

"I need to go to the bathroom." He abruptly announced and walked inside. Seconds later I heard the heavy thud of a door slamming, then silence. For a couple of minutes we stood there leaning against the railing, not speaking. With anyone else it would have been uncomfortable, and I'd be wracking my brain for words to fill the silence, but not with Ashley. My eyes darted between her oval, pale face and her hand resting less than an inch from mine. I itched to hold it.

Jesus Christ, was I afraid? Was that what this was about? Why on earth was I afraid of Ashley? I'd never been afraid of a woman before in my life, but she terrified me. Of all the women I'd known, and I couldn't remember the names of most, Ashley was the only one who made me sweat. She was such a proper lady, and always carried herself with a dignity I only dreamed of possessing. Maybe she was out of my league, and that was why… no, she'd definitely been turned on tonight. Hell, she asked to stay the night. Stop doubting yourself.

"Your brother's not coming back, is he?" Ashley murmured, then turned slightly in my direction. Her lips hovered over my neck, and it took all of my willpower not to take her hand and lead her to my bed. She'd kept me turned on all night rubbing up against me. When we danced I could smell her perfume, something deep and heady that made my head spin. And she kept pressing herself against me, and I could feel her breasts against mine. I had to remind myself not to let my hands slide down and cup her round ass, knowing if I did I might scare her off. When we were dancing, I felt her erect nipples through the thin fabric of her gown. I wanted to touch them, feel them, and taste those pink-brown nubs.

"I'd guess not." I said, realizing that Inky had pulled the rabbit out of his hat, the matchmaking magic in full strength, leaving us alone to work out this thing between us. Though I hoped it was Ashley's decision to throw herself into my arms, there was one little problem.

She was very drunk.

Ashley swiped her forehead with the back of her hand, her mouth half open and eyes wide and glassy. If this was anyone else, I'd be dragging them to the bedroom, but not Ashley. She'd had too much to drink, and as much as I wanted her, there was no way I'd take advantage of her in this state. I was completely screwed when it came to taking things slow with this woman. What I needed to do was get Ashley back to the safety of her own bed, saving her from my desire to rip the skimpy gown off her and revisit the lithe body I still remembered in my private fantasies.

"What are you thinking? You look so intense." Ashley whispered, then grabbed me by the waist and pulled me into her. Her foot stepped on mine and she stumbled, then crashed into me. Ashley shook her head back and forth and giggled.

"You okay, baby?" I asked, then placed my hands on her cheeks and gazed deep into her soulful green eyes. God, all I wanted to do was make love with her, but instead I whispered into her ear, "I'm going to take you back to your place."

Ashley laughed and pulled away, grabbing my hands at the same time. "I know you don't want to do that, Carly Poindexter. C'mon, give me the tour of your penthouse. All I've seen is the balcony, the bathroom, and your living room." Her smile was crooked, and I could see she was dropping all pretense that we were just friends reliving old times.

I bit my lip to keep from laughing. How our roles had reversed. The way Ashley was looking at me, she wanted more than just the grand tour. All I could think about was how to get her back to her own apartment, safe from my greedy mouth and hands.

"Are you sure you don't want me to walk you home? I think you've had too much to drink, and…"

Ashley laughed, then pulled me toward the sliding doors. As we stepped inside, she tripped and threw an arm around my shoulder to right herself.

"Oops." Ashley giggled, then she kicked off her heels. I should've persuaded her to step away from the bar a little earlier in the evening. What was left of the booze was on the far side of the living room, so I led her in the opposite direction toward the bedrooms. I had no intention of letting her into mine. That would be pushing my self-control to its limits. Instead, I hoped to steer Ashley toward one of the guest rooms.

"I want to see your bed." She giggled, then she fell against the wall outside my bedroom door. How she guessed it was mine was beyond me, but that was where she fell. Her laughter stopped, and she held her stomach.

"I don't feel so good." Ashley slurred, then glanced away, her face flushing. If I wasn't mistaken, her skin now glowed a subtle green. She turned back to me, and I noticed a speck of lipstick on her front teeth.

"C'mon Ashley, hold it in for just a minute, okay." I muttered, wanting to get her to the closest bathroom, which of course was in my bedroom. When I opened the door, Ashley practically fell through it, and then to my surprise she climbed onto my bed, laughing and patting the mattress beside her.

"Carly, come here." Ashley said in a sing-song voice, then she burst into laughter. All evidence of her feeling sick had disappeared, and I wondered if it hadn't been a ruse just to climb into my bed.

"Are you sure you feel alright, because you looked awful just a minute ago, babe." I stood in front of her with my hands on my hips, wanting to both take her in my arms and spank her, and not in the warm and friendly way.

"Don't tell me you've forgotten how to have sex in the last twenty years?" Ashley stretched out on the bed while my hormones surged. How the hell was I supposed to do this? If she woke up tomorrow and wondered what the hell I was doing with her naked, she'd flip out. I could virtually guarantee it, especially if she didn't remember anything. No way was I giving in to this temptation, not if she wasn't sober.

"Ashley, trust me, I've not forgotten how to make you hot,

but that's not the issue here. You've had too much to drink. Also, the first time I make love with you after all these years, I want you to remember it." While I talked she stood up, lifted her dress over her head, where it got stuck for a moment before she finally got it off, then she threw it across the room.

"Oh my God." I muttered, shaking my head.

Then, she reached behind her, and struggled to unhook her sheer black bra.

"Ashley, what are you doing? Babe, seriously, you are a sight for sore eyes, and I've wished for this moment ever since you came back into my life, but I'm not going to fuck it up doing something stupid like this."

She abandoned her bra and reached for her black lace panties, but then she fell back on the bed. Seeing her smooth skin presented to me like that made my brain momentarily shut off. I sat down next to her prone form and smoothed my trembling hand over her taut stomach.

"Carly, I know you want me, and I want you too. Now. Hell, if you won't go all the way, how about a little kiss, you know, for old times' sake?" Ashley propped herself up on her elbows and her green eyes swept over my body, starting at my face and slowly moving south. Her eyes clouded over, then she reached behind her again and the bra finally came loose.

Jesus, this woman was trying to kill me. Her breasts were the perfect size, not too big nor too small, and her hard little nipples beckoned to me. I wanted to lick them, kiss them while sliding my fingers into her hot, wet slit. Then, I'd slide down her body, rip her panties off, and taste her...

"Oh, fuck me." I sighed and swiped my mouth with the back of my hand. "Don't do it." My pussy clenched, and I knew my panties were likely soaking wet. But I wasn't touching her when she was in no condition to give me her consent.

"One kiss. That's it, Ashley James, only one, and then I'm

turning out this light and you are going to sleep here. I'm going to sleep in the guest room." My voice shook, and I realized one kiss might be more than I could handle. Fuck, I shouldn't be doing this. I was risking a future with this woman for a simple kiss, but then again, nothing had ever been simple with Ashley. I kicked off my heels and climbed on top of her, cupping her face in my hands. After all these years, it was no longer a fantasy. I stroked her pale cheeks and stared into those insane emerald eyes that had haunted my dreams for years.

"What are you waiting for?" Ashley whispered. Her hand stretched out, grabbing the back of my neck, then she squeezed it while guiding my lips until they hovered over hers. Our eyes locked, and every memory I had of the two of us in my bed during our one steamy summer together flashed through my mind, then my lips crashed into hers.

The taste of her mouth sent shock waves through me. It dissipated moments later as her tongue licked my closed lips, encouraging me to open to her. Ashley's tongue dipped inside, and a ragged moan rumbled through her chest. The hand on my neck pulled me down further, deepening the kiss. My groans mixed with hers, our breasts heaving against each other as our mouths explored what they'd been missing for so long. Reverent and soft at first, restrained passion transformed into primal need when I felt her other hand grab my ass. Ashley's lips left mine and connected to the sensitive skin under my ear, and my entire body shook with desire. My fingers found her now-tangled hair and pulled, then kneaded the thick blonde locks. Ashley's hips bucked, pressing her crotch against mine. Our bodies rocked together, and the friction of her pushing her pussy against mine was threatening to make me into the animal I was trying to avoid becoming. Ashley's lips found mine again, and it felt like she wanted to swallow me whole. If this went on much longer I'd let her.

God Almighty, where did she learn to kiss like this?

A little voice broke through in the back of my head, screaming for me to stop. I pulled back and her teeth took my bottom lip, gently tugging, wanting more. My heart felt like it would burst, and then, with lust still racing through my veins I rolled off of her and somehow ended up on the floor. I gasped for air, my body not quite ready to understand the common sense my brain was trying to hammer into it. Once I got my breathing under control, I picked myself up and stood over Ashley, who had the glazed look of a woman on the verge of either losing control or passing out. My inner voice echoed inside, urging me to leave now.

"I'm stepping out of the room for a few minutes." I muttered.

"Wait." Ashley pleaded, "I'm sorry."

"You did nothing wrong, Ashley, but if I don't leave now, I might do something we'll both regret."

———

"Carly, where have you been?" Ashley murmured as I shut the bedroom door behind me. I'd paced back and forth along the length of the balcony for the last ten minutes, bringing myself down from the dangerous high I'd felt minutes ago.

"Cooling off. How are you feeling?"

Ashley was under the blankets, her head propped up by pillows. Her now bloodshot eyes were half shut, and she had a serene smile stretched across her face.

"I'm thinking about our first kiss." Ashley patted the bed. "Come here." Her words were slurring even more than before. Instead of the bed, I sat on the chaise lounge by the window.

"Carly, did I ever tell you that when we first met I couldn't take my eyes off you? I mean, that first day of school you were the only girl I saw, and that I thought about you all day long?" She whispered, then yawned.

"No, you never did, but it was the same for me, Ashley, and I've never forgotten a single minute we've spent together since." I stretched out on the chaise, my feet hanging off the end. I glanced over at her and saw her eyes had closed, and wondered if she would remember anything about tonight. The dancing, the laughing, and the primal kiss that was like no other we'd shared before.

"I've missed you Ashley, so damn much." I whispered.

Her breathing slowed, and minutes later when I heard her softly snoring, I stood and gazed down at her, wondering how I'd ever survive if she didn't feel the same way I did.

This woman could destroy me. I'd never felt this way about anyone before, and if I was even remotely sane when it came to Ashley, I would leave her be, never bother her again. Protect my heart the way I always had, by ignoring it.

The urge to climb in bed and hold her tight was overwhelming, but how would she react in the morning to find my arms wrapped around her?

Instead of giving in to temptation, I kissed her forehead.

"I'm going to make you mine, Ashley James." I whispered, and reluctantly left to sleep alone in the guest room.

CHAPTER

Ten

ASHLEY

OH MY GOD, I felt like shit.

The pounding in my skull was unbelievable, and every muscle in my body was screeching at me for drinking gin like it was Kool-aid. A pillow was over my face, and when I removed it, I noticed a damp spot on the sheet where I must have been drooling. The heavy black curtains were shut, except for an inch or two, and even that amount of light forced me to hide under the blankets to block it out. Wait, a minute. The drapes I'd ordered for my bedroom hadn't arrived yet. Plus, they were yellow.

This wasn't my apartment.

"Knock knock." A soothing voice whispered, and instantly I knew where I was. Soft footsteps crossed the room, and I heard something being placed on the nightstand. I couldn't face Carly, so I kept the sheets over my head.

"I brought you some aspirin and a glass of water. Take your time getting up. I'm making you hangover food." Carly murmured, then I heard her feet padding away. When the door clicked shut, I exhaled, unaware I'd been holding my breath.

My memories of the prior night were fuzzy. I recalled dancing with Inky and meeting his friends. Oh, and Carly and I kissed—a lot.

"Did we get naked and do something I might regret?" I whispered.

This was worse than the time I got wasted at a frat party in college and woke up naked with a classmate. For months I wondered if anything had happened, especially because she was dating a football player who was in one of my classes. I didn't want it becoming public knowledge that I enjoyed both men and women, especially because I'd not been with a man yet, and still wanted to explore my sexuality. Turned out nothing had happened between us, but for a long time I was afraid I'd done something inappropriate with the girl, who'd only felt sorry for me and let me sleep in her bed.

My eyes fluttered open, and then I switched on the lamp next to the bed, wincing at the soft light. I lifted the sheet and saw the lacy black panties and bra I'd put on yesterday were still intact. Then I slid my hand under satin material and gingerly felt around. Everything felt normal, but this wasn't proof positive that nothing sexual had happened. Maybe we'd fooled around and I couldn't remember? It took all of my self-control not to throw myself at Carly every time I saw her, but so far I'd managed it. If I'd been drunk, I was damn sure I'd have found her irresistible.

I drew back the sheet and swung my legs over the side of the bed.

"Jesus, that hurts." I moaned, then I remembered the water and pain relievers. She had them on a black, shiny wooden tray. My hands shook as I scooped up the tablets, and moments later I chased them down with the contents of the entire glass, water dribbling down my chin.

"More water, now." I breathed, then looked around the

bedroom, praying there was a bathroom adjacent to it, so I didn't have to face the world outside these four walls. There were three doors to choose from, so I tiptoed to the nearest one and opened it to find the biggest closet I'd ever seen in my life. I shut it, crossed the room and tried another one. It opened onto a hallway, and I could smell coffee being brewed. My mouth watered, but I couldn't face Carly hung over wearing only my bra and panties. As I was closing the door I heard footsteps approaching, and Carly whistling softly.

I scrambled to the bed and drew the blankets over me, just as she strolled into the room.

"Hey, Ashley, I brought you a big carafe of water, plus coffee and toast." Carly murmured, placing another tray on the nightstand, and grabbing the other one. "You feeling okay?"

"I feel like hell, but I'll survive." Unable to look her in the eye, I reached for the carafe with trembling fingers. Carly placed her tapered fingers on mine and I pulled my hand back.

"I've got this." Carly filled the glass and held it out for me. I drank it down in less than thirty seconds, and I would swear it was the best water I'd had in my life. Carly took the glass from me and refilled it. I downed it faster than the first.

"More?" Carly held up the carafe, and I shook my head, then pointed at the coffee. After a couple of sips, I placed it back on the tray, and finally met Carly's gaze.

"I'm really sorry. Was I a complete mess in front of everyone?" I muttered, praying I had done nothing stupid to embarrass her in front of the other guests.

"Nope. All the crazy shit happened after they left. Oh, and it wasn't as bad as you think. You want to take a shower while I finish making breakfast? It might make you feel better." Carly's hand lifted, and for a moment I thought she was reaching for me. Instead it fell back to her lap.

"The bathroom is right over there." She stood and pointed

to the one door I hadn't tried. "Hope you like pancakes." She grinned, then padded out of the bedroom. When she opened the door, I could smell bacon frying, and my stomach churned. I knew greasy food was good for a hangover, but I was nervous about being able to keep anything down.

When I got out of bed this time, I looked for any evidence that Carly had slept there too. The sheets, blankets and pillows were all over the place, so I couldn't tell. It mortified me that I'd have to break down and ask her what actually happened. With anyone else I would've thrown on my clothes and run out, not worrying about appearances. Not with Carly though, because maybe, just maybe, I wished we'd actually done something, and the naughtier the better.

———

I was going to put my clothes on from last night, but the food smelled too good, so I threw on a robe that was hanging on the bathroom door. It looked like a man's robe, black with red piping. When I walked into the kitchen, Carly began to say something, but then her mouth snapped shut. The coffee she was pouring overflowed the cup.

"Shit!"

I couldn't help but laugh, which hurt like hell, because my head was still pounding. A roll of paper towels was on the counter next to me, so I tore off a few sheets and handed them to her. While she mopped up the mess, Carly glanced my way, biting her lower lip.

"You look so sexy in my robe. Uh, sorry about this." Carly gestured to where she'd spilled the coffee, then tossed the towels in the trash can under the sink. "Let me start again." She poured me a cup and handed it to me with a sheepish grin. It was funny to see her blush, something I knew she rarely did.

"Need any help?" I asked. She shook her head and pointed me toward the dining room. Carly followed moments later and set a tray filled with bacon, eggs, pancakes, and syrup on the table. This time my tummy churned with hunger instead of nausea.

"Thanks." I said, and loaded up my plate. Carly was silent. She sipped her orange juice and watched as I made an absolute pig of myself. After last night, I was past the point of embarrassment. When I was done, I piled my dishes on the tray and started for the kitchen.

"You don't have to do that." Carly took the tray out of my hands. When she got to the kitchen she began loading the dishwasher. I picked up a sponge from the sink and was about to start on the counters when she stopped me.

"Please, I've got this. You're my guest."

"I'm surprised you don't have a maid." I teased. I'd had no idea how successful Carly really was, until last night when I discovered she owned the building and lived in the penthouse. Carly had never once let on that she was wealthy, her demeanor being so down to earth. Hell, her art collection alone must have been worth a healthy chunk of change. Suspicion took hold of my mind; Carly Poindexter could have any woman she wanted, so why the hell did she want me? And why was I resisting?

"I do. Ruthie works Mondays, Wednesdays, and Fridays. I can manage by myself on the other days." Carly replied, a smile starting to spread across her cheeks, but then she glanced away.

"Why don't you have a girlfriend?" I blurted, instantly regretting my question. It was none of my business, but it made not a lick of sense. Carly was gorgeous, had a curvy body that was off the charts hot, and was worth a fortune.

"Because, I've never wanted one before, unless I count what

we had all those years ago." She murmured, and I felt something fluttering in my stomach.

"Carly, you don't have to be alone if you don't want to be. I bet you could snap your fingers and get almost anyone you wanted. What's wrong with this picture?"

"Just because I don't have a girlfriend, or have ever contemplated having one, until now, doesn't mean anything is wrong with me. My focus has been on building my business. It doesn't mean I've been a nun, far from it. I've preferred to keep things casual." Carly shut the dishwasher and leaned back against it. A dark curl fell on her forehead, and I felt a moist heat begin to burn between my legs.

"Ashley, you told me about your botched wedding, and that you were never in love with that guy. You could have a second career as a model, and I believe if you snapped your fingers, men and women would line up around the building to get in your pants, so what's holding you back?"

I shrugged my shoulders and felt my knees growing weak. Fear held me back, but I wasn't sharing that with her yet. Carly's face grew dark for a moment, then she picked up a rag and started wiping the counter. Moments later, words rushed out of her in a torrent.

"You came on to me last night, Ashley. You're also the one who initiated our first kiss after we had dinner at Beasley's. What that tells me is you're afraid. Of what, I'm not exactly sure." She threw the rag to the side, and faced me. "You still want to have sex? Because if that's all you can handle right now, I'm prepared to keep it light, no strings attached." Carly blushed and put her hands behind her back, thrusting her breasts out. I knew what my answer was going to be, but I felt like she had the upper hand, and wasn't sure if I liked that. Carly shared no secrets, yet I'd told her a few.

"I'm sorry about last night, about coming on to you. I

shouldn't have drunk so much, but was nervous about, well, everything." I threw my hands up for a second, then glanced away.

"Don't be. I mean, it's not as if I didn't want you to." Carly said, a sly grin spreading across her cheeks. Suddenly, I was incensed. She'd seen me vulnerable, at my very worst. Since we'd reentered each other's lives, I'd told her the gory details of my past. Carly held the advantage, and my mouth opened before I could think first.

"Do you abuse animals?" I asked. Carly's arched eyebrows drew together.

"No."

"Do you like to kick people when they're down? Are there any skeletons in your closet I should know about?" I bit off, then her eyes darkened. Carly began to speak, but I attacked even more.

"I've told you my deepest secrets, about Harvard and my fucked-up wedding. It's not fair that I've shared my secrets, but I have none of yours. Have you ever committed a crime? You know, stolen something, or assaulted another person?" I inched closer to her, hoping she'd confess something, anything, so I didn't feel so much like… damaged goods?

"Not that I'm aware of. Why are you asking me these questions?" Carly crossed her arms over her chest. "I have a feeling your ex ruined your ability to trust, and I must say, I don't blame you. Being dumped at the altar must've hurt."

I allowed a few seconds to pass, shrugged my shoulders, and responded, "I don't know why I'm asking them. Maybe to change the subject? I guess I'm a little afraid of you, or more importantly, of us. I don't think I can have a serious relationship with anyone right now, but I'd be a liar if I said I didn't find you attractive. So, yes, Carly Poindexter, I want to have sex with you." I breathed, then closed the distance between us and wrapped my arms around her long neck.

Carly's back straightened, and her dark eyes bored into mine. She licked her full lips and inched forward. I was about to lean in and kiss her, seal the deal so to speak, when she placed her hands on my shoulders and gently pushed. Her next words shocked me, but I was also impressed.

"Let's spend the day together first."

CHAPTER
Eleven

CARLY

AFTER STOPPING by Ashley's apartment, so she could change into a pair of jeans and a simple flowery blouse, I drove us to the site where our relationship began all those years ago.

"I haven't been to the Raleigh Rose Garden since the last time we were here, back in high school." Ashley's head slowly turned, taking in the elegance of the flower beds. It was so quiet, hard to believe the Raleigh Little Theater and the university were only a few yards away. Vibrant pink, red, and orange blooms shone under the afternoon sun. "It's even more stunning than I remember."

I didn't speak, wondering if Ashley recalled what we did the last time we'd come here. I'd brought her to the gardens for a reason, hoping to stir up memories of that long-ago day. During spring break, while everyone else in our class vacationed at the beach, we'd spent the week together exploring the city. This garden was where we'd first exchanged those three magic words. I felt like a teenager again, reliving the same gut-wrenching anxieties I struggled with in my senior year. Summoning the courage to confess how I really felt for her the first time wreaked havoc on my emotions. I feared nothing, except rejection. Twenty years later, and I still ached to hold her and never let go, yet the same fear persisted. But if all Ashley wanted was a casual fling, I'd have to honor that.

"Let's sit. I want to enjoy the scenery." Ashley said, then astounded me by reaching for my hand and guiding me to a bench. There was a small pond in front of it, and brightly colored koi swam up to the surface, mouths opening and shutting. It was tough to focus on our surroundings, because a single thought kept dancing through my mind.

Ashley was holding my hand.

"Do you remember what happened here?" Ashley turned to me and whispered. Was it a trick question? I thought we weren't supposed to be romantic, though holding my hand seemed at odds with her wish to keep things casual. Should I say yes, that I'd never, ever forgotten the first time I'd told her I loved her? Or should I feign ignorance, keeping it light, so it wouldn't seem like I was pressing too hard? I didn't want to freak her out now that her long, delicate fingers were intertwined with mine.

"Of course." I murmured, glancing away. "How could I ever forget?" My eyes couldn't meet hers, because I was afraid she'd see much more than simple lust etched into my features. Ashley's fingers touched my cheek, turning my face until her emerald-green eyes settled on mine.

"Carly, I know I've been hard to reach, unable to commit to much, but that doesn't mean I don't remember what we had." Ashley gazed around the pond before her eyes locked with mine once more. "I've never forgotten what took place on this bench all those years ago. No one had ever said they loved me before." Ashley almost looked the same as she did then, except her skin glowed more now, and her face was thinner, more regal, not baby-soft like it once was. There were crinkles at the corners of her eyes, but instead of making Ashley appear older, they added a mature sexiness that made me weak at the knees.

"Wanna do it again? You know, kiss your ex-girlfriend for old times' sake?" Damn it, what the hell had happened to me? If this was anyone else, I would have dragged her back to my apartment for a tumble between the sheets, but with Ashley, I sensed she craved intimacy and sincerity.

"Yes, I'd like nothing more than to kiss you." The way she bit her bottom lip after saying that made my blood heat up. The surrounding gardens disappeared from view when Ashley took my hand in hers and pulled me closer. Then, just like that long-ago afternoon, she shut her eyes. I leaned into her and cupped her face in my palms, letting my lips glance over hers like I did back then. Years ago, I didn't know what the hell I was doing. I knew there was more to it than lips touching, but when I was a teenager, I worried about fucking it up, so I kept it simple. Drawing back from her, Ashley's eyes opened, wet and glassy. Her lips parted, but instead of kissing her again, I took us back to that far-off day.

"Mom and Dad are going to some fancy shindig at the country club tonight, so we'll have the place to ourselves. Maybe we could play video games and, you know, fool around. Do you think your folks will let you come over?" I whispered. Ashley grabbed my hand and placed it on the curve of her breast.

"There's a payphone in the parking lot. I pissed them off, because I missed curfew last night, and I thought they were going to ground me. I'll butter Mom up, tell her I'll do all the laundry for the next week." Ashley wrapped her arms around my neck and pulled me in tight. Her breath was hot against my skin, and then I felt her tongue playing with my ear, nibbling on the lobe. I shivered, waves of sensation pulsing between my legs when she blew in my ear. Placing my hands on her shoulders, I lightly pushed her back.

"Ashley, if I don't get you naked in my bed soon, I will die of…" My words dried in my mouth, and Ashley got to her feet and reached for my hand.

"Well, we can't have that, can we?"

———

It terrified me, the thought that I'd disappoint her. While other women had generally applauded my prowess in bed, Ashley was different. I wanted more than just a tumble in the sheets, despite telling her this was a no-strings-attached romp. The only way I'd break down the walls between us was if I truly made love to her, and I hadn't made love to anyone since she left Raleigh twenty years ago.

In the elevator, I kept my distance, stuffing my hands in my pockets. By the time we arrived on the top floor, Ashley was giving me funny looks.

The keys fell to the floor as I attempted to open the door. "Sorry." I mumbled, then Ashley bent down to pick them up. I couldn't keep my eyes off that full, round ass I'd been craving since the moment I saw her. With a steadier hand than mine, she fitted the key in the lock.

"After you." Ashley gestured, so I led her inside. When I turned to close the door, she was less than a foot away, blocking me.

"Are you still a goddess underneath the sheets?" Ashley said, then pressed herself against me. "I've got a secret I want to share." She whispered, then she kissed the tender skin beneath my ear.

"Yes," I murmured, relishing the feel of her fingers stroking the hair on the back of my neck.

"For twenty years, I've always compared my lovers to you." She pulled back, gazing into my eyes. "And no one ever turned me on the way you used to."

"Even your fiancé?" I asked, pulling her in close. Shit, why the hell did I have to bring him up? It was like inviting a stranger into my bed for a three-way I didn't want.

Ashley stiffened for a moment, then she murmured in my ear, "Yes. In fact, if I knew he wouldn't be able to make me orgasm, all I had to do was recall your magic fingers and your tongue." She pulled back and bit her lip. "The memory of you made me come every single time."

My heart stopped beating for a moment, and Ashley winked. "Close your mouth, Carly, before a bug flies in."

I blushed, and a tiny giggle escaped my lips.

"Unless you want to make love in the entry foyer, why don't we move on to your bedroom." Ashley tilted her head to the side, then grabbed my arms and pulled me into her chest. Her lips found mine while I willed myself to stay upright. My legs were trembling so much I feared I'd fall over. My mouth opened, and her tongue dipped inside. I felt Ashley's nipples through her blouse, pressing insistently against mine. She groaned into my mouth, then pulled back and took my hand.

"Your bedroom... Now, Carly." Ashley's voice had an edge to it, and the heat between my legs grew almost unbearable.

"Yes, now." I mumbled, then I turned around and led her down the long hallway to my room. When we got to the door, I froze, suddenly aware that in all my wildest fantasies, I never expected this stunning woman to share my bed again.

"Are you okay?" Ashley whispered. "Because, baby, I need you."

My mouth opened and nothing came out, then with a trembling hand I turned the doorknob and gestured for her to walk in ahead of me. My heart was pounding, and as she brushed by me, I could smell her unique scent, floral, with a hint of musk. Ashley strolled up to my bed, spun around, then lifted her blouse over her head, and dropped it to the floor.

"Can you help me with this?" She turned, held her hair up, and for a second I didn't know what she wanted. Then I realized it was her bra she wanted help with. I cleared my throat and walked over. The soft pink lacy garment made her creamy skin appear whiter. I'd always loved women who wore sexy lingerie, but more than that, I preferred them on my floor. With shaky fingers, I unhooked the clasp, and Ashley lifted her arms so I could remove it. I dropped it to the ground, then cupped a full breast in each hand from behind.

"Yes." Ashley hissed, and my fingers found her erect nipples. She backed into my embrace while I gently squeezed, making sure not to squeeze too hard. She groaned, a deep sound I'd only remembered in my fantasies. "I want you so bad, Carly."

"Turn around," I said, and let go of her breasts. She faced me, draping her arms over my shoulders.

"Too many clothes, Carly." She whispered, then she unbuttoned my blouse, taking her time with each button. Her fingers trembled, and I resisted the urge to rip the garment off. I wasn't wearing a bra, and when the green satin material brushed over my nipples, a shiver raced down my spine. When it was off, my blouse joined Ashley's bra on the floor.

My heart thundered as we stared at each other, the tension between us building. This perfect woman actually wanted me, and for the first time in recent memory, I was terrified. Ashley was my kryptonite, the perfect poison who could either make me complete or rip my heart to shreds. And while I might be afraid, Ashley never looked so confident, her eyes boldly meeting mine.

"Your breasts are so beautiful, Carly." Ashley stepped

forward, then bent over and took a nipple in her mouth. Electricity raced through me. Then she let go of it and smiled. "You still resemble a goddess after all these years, both soft and muscular." She stepped back and undid the zipper on her jeans.

"Let me take them off." I murmured and dropped to my knees. "I've wanted to taste you since you walked back into my life."

Moments later, Ashley stepped out of the jeans and kicked them away. "Sit down, and spread your legs as wide as you can."

She sat on the edge of the bed, but when I went to spread her legs open, I sensed a sudden shyness on her part. I stroked her inner thigh, barely able to take my eyes off her beautiful pussy.

"Open those legs wide for me, Ashley." I murmured. She reached out and combed her fingers through my hair, then slowly her legs parted. I could smell her arousal and saw how wet she was. My mouth watered, and I couldn't believe I was about to taste her again. I stroked her inner thigh, and I heard Ashley's breathing quicken. Her legs opened more, then I leaned down and licked her pussy, starting at the bottom, all the way up to the top.

"Carly," Ashley hissed, and I continued to lick from one end of her to the other, then I flicked her swollen clit with my tongue. "Oh my God," Ashley fell back on the mattress, fingers clutching my hair while I sucked on her engorged clit. Her hips bucked, and she continued to moan my name, over and over. I felt a tear sliding down my cheek and hoped Ashley wouldn't notice. I pushed her thighs further apart, then glanced up, and said, "I want to taste everything you have to give, make you come for me, Ashley."

Ashley trembled. Then, I worked my tongue back to her

engorged clit. I slid two fingers inside of her, and I reached down and slid my other hand into my slacks. I was so wet, and when my fingers brushed over my clit, I groaned into her pussy.

"Come on my tongue, babe." I murmured, the vibrations of my words directly against her clit. Ashley's fingers dug into my hair, and I removed my hand from my pussy and placed one hand on each of her hips, holding her in place while my tongue worked its magic, then I curled my fingers inside of her, and increased the suction.

"Jesus, Carly, you're going to make me come." Ashley's voice was so high, it almost sounded like a screech, and then an orgasm tore through her, so hard it bordered on violence. Her frame shook as I massaged the sensitive spot inside of her, and I didn't stop until Ashley's fingers let go of my hair. Her inner thighs were wet, then I kissed her clit, and she shuddered in response.

"Come here," Ashley murmured, so I stood, removed the rest of my clothing, then lay down next to her. She turned her head to the side and a languid smile spread across her cheeks. Our eyes locked. Ashley climbed on top of me and took one of my hard nipples in her mouth. My back arched, and a groan escaped me. Then, she moved up, her full lips hovering over mine. "You're even better than I remember, Carly, and more beautiful, too."

The smell of our arousal filled the air, and my pussy was so wet it bordered on embarrassing. Ashley's gaze was smoky, filled with a passion I'd never seen in any of my prior partners. The connection between us was so real, and so strong. How could I get Ashley to feel it, too?

Ashley's lips brushed over mine, then I felt her tongue seek admission. My mouth opened, and for several heated minutes we kissed while she pressed against my slit with her thighs.

Pressure built inside of me, and I craved more than her leg. Suddenly, she pulled away, and an involuntary whimper escaped me.

"Patience." Ashley whispered, and her mouth dropped back down to my breasts, licking oh-so-close to my nipples, but never touching them. Frustration built inside of me. Between her thigh pressing against my pussy, and her teasing mouth on my breasts, I thought I would pass out. "I want all of you Carly."

"Please, Jesus, take all of me, I'm yours." I gasped as her lips finally wrapped around my nipple. Like her kissing, Ashley was intent on making this last. Never had my breasts been so lavished by anyone's mouth, and then she slid down and stopped moving.

"What?" I breathed, so close to my climax, yet so far away.

"You're beautiful, and so very, very wet." Ashley said, and I detected a hint of wonder in her voice.

"It's all your fault." My voice quaked. "All of this is your doing."

"And now I get to taste you." Ashley said, then I felt her tongue dancing around my folds, hitting every inch of skin except my clit. Was that her goal, to keep me on the edge until I exploded with desire? Finally, her mouth made contact, and my hands clutched the blankets, and a high-pitched whine came from my throat. Ashley slid a finger inside me, and I heard a sharp sob and wondered where it came from, then realized it was me.

"You're so close, baby, so damned close." Ashley muttered, her mouth leaving my pussy for a second.

"Please, Ashley, faster. I can't..." My mouth snapped shut when her lips wrapped around my clit, then they were gone, and she was licking my inner thighs. "Oh my God, I..."

Her tongue returned, and two fingers slid inside, curling up in just the right spot. My body went rigid, and my eyes snapped shut as ecstasy crashed through me. The sensations were chaotic, and my heart was pounding in my chest. I felt bare, exposed even, and in that instant I knew my love for her had never died. Instead, it had been reawakened by the beautiful woman I'd dreamed of for most of my life.

Normally I felt anxious after an orgasm like that, but when Ashley moved up my body and laid her head on my chest, I continued to breathe, slowly regaining my composure. My legs shifted, and I wondered if I'd ever been so wet for another woman before in my life.

"I'm giving you five minutes." Ashley murmured.

"Five minutes?"

"Yes," Ashley looked up at me, her eyes half-hooded. "Until I make love to you again, my beautiful Carly."

CHAPTER

Twelve

CARLY

HOURS PASSED and Ashley's head remained on my chest, her arm flung over my stomach. I shifted slightly so I wouldn't wake her, one of my legs tingling from being in the same place for too long. Contentment washed through me as I listened to the gentle sound of her breathing. Ashley's eyes danced under her lids, and I wondered what she was dreaming about, if perhaps she ever dreamed about me?

Fuck.

How could I keep things light now that she'd walked back into my life? For years I'd never been interested in anything more than casual sex, but with Ashley I was unsure I could keep things strings-free. My eyes fluttered shut, and I recalled the vow, that idealistic promise we'd made to each other that long-ago night when we went our separate ways.

"In ten years' time, if we both are still single, let's meet at our high school reunion, and maybe we can…"

"I promise you, Carly, in ten years we will be together, though I don't know how I'm going to wait so long."

Was it possible I was still in love with her?

When you were a kid, ten years seemed like a lifetime, but now that twenty years had passed, it felt like only yesterday that my heart was torn into a million tiny pieces. A tear coursed down my cheek, and I swiped at it with the back of my hand. Fuck me, this was the second time she'd made me cry since she'd returned. I hadn't shed any tears since that night ten years ago, and here I was becoming a crybaby whenever she was around. Since the moment I'd seen Ashley at the hospital when Dad was sick, I'd been wrecked, to the point I barely recognized myself any longer.

If this had been one of my usual casual encounters, I would have offered them a warm towel and shown them the door by now, but this wasn't just anybody. Ashley had the power to either complete me, or utterly demolish the life I'd created for myself. But, if all she wanted was a sexual thing, friends with benefits, or whatever they called it nowadays, I was game. However, I couldn't stop hoping that she felt the same way for me that I felt for her.

My eyelids grew heavy. I hated to do it, but now my other leg was cramping, so I carefully turned over, praying I wouldn't wake Ashley.

"I'm not asleep, Carly. You okay?" She yawned, then wrapped her arm around me and kissed my back.

I debated whether I should tell her the truth. Would Ashley freak out if she knew how I actually felt? No, I couldn't risk it.

"I'm okay, just reminiscing. Thinking about our school days, that's all." I squeezed her hand and held it against my breasts. My heart thumped underneath, and I hoped she didn't notice it ramping up.

"Oh, I hated high school. When I transferred there for junior year, I thought it would be miserable, filled with the usual high-school cliques. Then, I met you, and everything changed." Ashley murmured, her breath tickling the hairs on the back of my head.

"Did I ever tell you about flunking that Latin test on purpose?" I snickered.

"What are you talking about?"

"You were the new kid, acing all of your papers. I knew Mr. Creighton would get you to tutor me, you know, to help you make friends. I'd tutored a classmate the year before, so I figured he'd do the same thing. Plus, I was a straight-A student, so it freaked him out that I'd flunked a test... oh, and I skipped out on some homework too. That's how I got us quality time alone in the school library." I laughed. Damn, I was a determined kid. Ashley laughed too, thank God. For a moment I worried she'd think I'd been a stalker since day one.

"Whatever Carly wants, she gets, right?" Ashley tightened her grip on me, and I felt soft kisses on my back. Fuck it, maybe I could take this further than I thought.

"You know what else I remember? That promise we made to each other, while strolling around Lake Johnson." I murmured, and waited for a response. When I got none, I continued, "If ten or so years passed and we were both still single, we'd find each other. I promised you I'd wait forever. Now it's been twenty years." I whispered the last sentence, and when she didn't respond, my gut twisted into a knot.

Shit. My fucking big mouth was getting me in trouble again, scaring her off.

I waited for Ashley to speak, and every second stretched into an eternity. I fully expected her to leap out of the bed and race for the door.

Instead, the sound of her soft snores put my nerves at rest. Thank God she hadn't heard me. I settled back on the pillow and closed my eyes, our first kiss playing over and over in my mind.

———

The sunrise woke me from a dead sleep, so I leapt out of bed to shut the drapes, hoping she wasn't awakened by the light. When I turned around, I realized I shouldn't have bothered.

Ashley was gone.

CHAPTER

Thirteen

ASHLEY

"IF TEN OR so years passed, and we were both still single, we'd find each other. I promised you I'd wait forever. Now it's been twenty years." Carly's voice trailed off, and I froze.

The night was perfect. Romantic and sexy fun, just what the doctor ordered, but then Carly had to bring up The Promise. Oh my God, I hadn't thought of that in years, though of course I'd never forgotten it.

When I was kicked out of Harvard Medical School, that promise kept me going as I struggled to move forward with my life. If all else failed, maybe Carly would be the pot of gold at the end of the rainbow. I grappled with the decision to move home with my tail between my legs, but decided against it. How could I face the humiliation of being booted out of one of the finest universities in the world? What would my friends and family say? Would Carly be ashamed of me, shun me for being a loser? Or even worse, had she moved on with somebody else?

But, life carried on, and eventually I found a way through the pain. I dated other people, had crushes, almost married a rich doctor for all the wrong reasons. The promise was real. It represented the love we had, and that we would always have for each other, even if it was in the distant future. Now that future was here, and it scared the hell out of me.

Carly shifted, and I thought she might be waiting for my response. God help me, I faked snoring, hoping she'd stop bringing up the past, which was rapidly becoming the present. I knew she wasn't proposing marriage, but it sounded like she wanted to take our friends-with-benefits situation and elevate it to a higher level, and I wasn't prepared for that. Once I was sure she was asleep, I'd escape. As amazing as it was to feel her arms around me, to make love with her again after all these years, I couldn't handle anything serious with her, or anyone else.

———

"Somebody looks like they stayed up all night. Hope it was fun." Mark elbowed me in the side and smirked. I could feel blood rushing to my face, and Mark bit his lip to keep from laughing.

"It was… fun." Hell, there was no way I could forget it. I was in a daze, because of last night. Mind-blowing sex had that effect on me. Of course, that was tempered by the text message I'd received from Carly this morning. She said she was sorry if she made me uncomfortable, that she wanted to make it up to me.

That made me wince.

I hadn't replied, not knowing what to say. Despite my reservations, I didn't want to hurt her. Carly was my first love, and even if she made me want to bang my head against the wall with her headstrong ways, causing her pain was not on my agenda.

"You're a fast worker. Was it that looker who came to see you last week?"

"Jesus, Mark. What's up with all the questions? Yes, I was with her."

"Sorry. Jeez, you're touchy today. Just moved back to Raleigh and you've already got yourself a girlfriend. Wish I could be so lucky." Mark muttered. I faked a laugh, then we were confronted by the arrival of a young mother with her son.

"Please, you gotta help my baby. A bunch of thugs beat him up. I think his arm is broken." Tears coursed down her cheeks, though I could tell she was trying to keep it together for her child's sake. He couldn't have been more than twelve years old, his somber face hiding his pain. Both were trying to be strong for the other, and it wasn't working.

"I'll take him to the examination room. Mark, would you mind getting her information?" I asked, then crouched in front of the youngster.

"It's going to be alright. What's your name?"

"Hugo. Hugo Alvarez." He tilted his chin up defiantly, but I noticed his eyes were red and glassy, one almost swollen shut. Not only was his arm possibly broken, but he had a black eye, and a bloody crust was forming around his nostrils.

"We're going to get you cleaned up, and I'll get the doctor to see you as soon as possible. I want you to follow me now, Hugo, okay?"

———

"You're a lucky young man." Doctor Spruill said. "One of your bones, the ulna, had a clean break. Most likely it won't require resetting, but you will be wearing that sling for a few weeks. Ms. James here will send you home with instructions on home care."

"Thank you, sir." Hugo replied, and the doctor left. His mother burst into tears again, reached out to hug him, then stopped, afraid of hurting her boy.

"Oh, baby, don't ever get in the way of a bunch of bullies like that again. Run, crawl, do whatever it takes to get away." The mother, Jenny Alvarez, was distraught over much more than her son's arm though. Before I brought her back to the examination room, she asked me about the bill, and from the look in her eye I knew it was going to be an issue.

"I'm going to see to your paperwork and will be back in a flash. You two stay here while I get things taken care of." Mrs. Alvarez gingerly wrapped her arms around Hugo as I left the room. I needed to get their forms ready, but I also needed Mark's help. I was still new, and unfamiliar with any programs the hospital had for patients who struggled financially. It was obvious the woman would do anything for her son, and it tore me up inside to think money stood in the way of Hugo getting the best care possible.

"Mark, are you with someone right now?" He shook his head no.

"I need your help with that mother and son who came in with the broken arm. From what Mrs. Alvarez said, they are struggling financially and I don't know enough about hospital policy to…"

"I've got it. Get their paperwork together, oh, and you're going to need this too." He reached under the counter, then placed a form on the stack I already had. "Come with me, so you can learn what to say the next time this happens." Mark walked briskly to the exam room with me hurrying to keep up.

"Mrs. Alvarez?" Mark said, when he opened the blue curtain.

"Yes, but you can call me Jenny." She held out her hand which Mark shook.

"Hugo, I'm going to borrow your mother for a few minutes. Will you be okay on your own?" He asked. The boy nodded, and we left. Mark led us to the empty gray office at the end of the corridor.

"Normally someone from finance would go over this with you, but seeing that you've been through so much already I'm not going to make you wait. Ashley told me you had concerns about the bill." He said once the three of us were seated. She nodded, then brushed a tear away. Poor woman's eyes were so swollen it had to be painful.

"We have several options to help you. UNC Rex Hospital takes pride in treating everyone regardless of their ability to pay. What I'm going to do is set you up with an appointment to speak with a social worker who will help you with financial arrangements. Is it okay for me to do that?"

She nodded, her back straightening. I sensed she was uncomfortable talking about her finances.

"Hugo is enrolled in Medicaid, and I get him regular checkups through the city health department. I do my best to keep my boy healthy. What on earth was he thinking getting in the middle of that mess?" She shook her head and put her face in her hands for a moment, taking a couple of deep breaths.

"Is this the best number where we can reach you?" Mark asked, a note of concern in his voice. Jenny nodded, and her left leg bounced up and down from nerves.

"I will take care of it on my end. You will be contacted in one to three days to inform you about the appointment I'm setting up with the social worker. Now if you could sign these forms…" Mark spoke in a steady, calm voice as he explained all she needed to do to keep Hugo's arm comfortable at home, and about the financial aid programs. Mark impressed me with his caring professionalism. By the time he was through she managed a small smile, then asked where the nearest bus stop was.

I was nearing the end of my shift, and something about Jenny and Hugo touched me. This woman was trying so damn hard to be the best mom she could be, and it must seem like the world was throwing every obstacle it could in her path.

"I'm about to leave myself. Would you like a ride?" I blurted out. Mark raised an eyebrow, but Jenny turned to me with the first real smile I'd seen from her since she arrived.

"Oh, if it's no trouble, that would be wonderful."

"Give me twenty minutes and I'll get you both home." I glanced at her address on the form. It was only ten minutes from my place downtown. "You're practically right down the street from me. It's no trouble at all."

———

Jenny and Hugo lived off Capital Boulevard in a rundown apartment building called the Millbrook Arms. When they got out of the car, the door to the rental office flew open and a tall man with shoulder-length gray hair ran over.

"There you are. I've been worried sick about you." The man cried. Jenny flew into his arms while Hugo stood back respectfully.

"Mr. Turner, you have no idea what we've..."

"I know exactly what you've been through. Those men who've been sabotaging the building beat the crap out of Hugo." The man crouched down in front of the boy and examined his broken arm.

"You were very brave confronting those men, but don't you dare do that again. Mrs. Hernandez in 2C called me right after it happened. She saw the whole thing, told me you saw them sneaking around the back to the basement. Said they had a big saw with them. They were bad men, but it's not your responsibility to fight them. Next time, you run away and then call the police." He stood up and sighed. Then, he noticed me leaning against my car.

"You're wearing scrubs. Did you help this young man today?"

"Yes, I gave them a ride home from the hospital. Sounds like Hugo here is a brave guy, but I'm with you. He should never, ever fight with a bunch of grown men. What's going on? Were they burglars?" I replied, curious as to why grown men would beat on a kid.

"A few months ago, a real estate developer made me an offer to buy this place. I refused. This place is home for so many people I'm proud to call my friends. Since then I've had my basement flooded, the furnace broke down, though it was only two years old, and the electrical boxes were overloaded. They've made four offers, each better than the last, but I've turned them all down. Every time I say no, another so-called accident happens. A man with the real-estate agency was here last week, and of course the thugs came back. These shady developers are trying to run us out of the neighborhood to build more of their overpriced lofts and fancy nightclubs. I'm not selling, no matter what they do." He turned and addressed Hugo again. "I'm telling you once more. If you see some shady characters around here, hide. They know who you are now, kid." Hugo shrugged his shoulders and turned to his mom.

"Can we have Chinese takeout for dinner? I'm starving."

Jenny's face collapsed for a brief second, then she mustered a smile. After her talk with Mark earlier about finances, I had a feeling she would have to tell him no. After the day he'd had, I thought he deserved a treat.

"Actually, I'm hungry too. Point me to the nearest takeout and I'll get you whatever you want."

"No, you don't have to do that!" Jenny exclaimed, and I saw her eyes fill up with tears again. The woman had been through it today, and I felt my eyes getting wet too.

"I insist. Hugo deserves it, and so do you. So, what can I get for you both?"

———

"Aunt Dotty. What are you doing here?" My aunt surprised me by pulling into the parking lot of the Chinese restaurant as I was getting out of my car.

"Happy Family has the best WonTon soup in Raleigh. I'm hungry, what else would I be doing here?" She hugged me. "This is a little out of your way. How'd you find out about it?"

I explained to her about what happened with the Alvarez family. She'd worked as a community activist for years, and her eyes dimmed as she heard about what Hugo had gone through.

"Those assholes." She said, taking me by surprise. I'd never heard her curse before. "The same thing happens all over town, whenever those rich sons of bitches drive poorer families out of their homes. Gentrification is a fancy name for kicking out the 'undesirables.' Then they have the nerve to complain about the homeless. How the hell do they think some of the homeless became that way in the first place?" She grabbed me by the arm and dragged me into the restaurant. "I'm taking care of this. What are they eating?"

Half an hour later the two of us delivered their dinners. We found the Alvarez family and Mr. Turner on a playground behind the building. They were waiting for us at an old picnic table, its green paint peeling off. Jenny greeted us shyly as we approached.

"My son and I appreciate all you've done for us today." She took a bag from my hand and set it down. "People like you give us hope. That's hard to come by nowadays. Hugo, run inside and wash up before you eat. Oh, and be careful with…" By the time she got to the end of her sentence he was inside the building. Jenny laughed and shook her head. "He's a handful, but he's my everything."

Aunt Dotty and I placed the other bags on the table, and Mr. Turner helped.

"My name is Dotty. I ran into my niece at Happy Family, the Chinese place." She introduced herself to Mr. Turner, who shook her hand for a second longer than usual.

"Billy Turner. I own the place. I assume your niece told you about what's been going on here. Hugo was a brave fool today, but I have to admit if more people would stick up for what's right, this world would be a better place." Aunt Dotty beamed, and if my eyes weren't deceiving me, she was blushing.

I took a closer look at Billy, then at her, wondering if a love connection was happening in front of my eyes. Once they filled their plates they sat next to each other, neither saying much, but that didn't last for long. Minutes later their food remained untouched as they talked passionately about corruption at City Hall.

"Jenny," I said, after finishing my meal. "This is my phone number. If you need anything at all please call me." I scribbled my number on an old business card I found in my wallet. "And, I'm not just saying that. If Hugo needs a ride to a doctor's appointment, or you just need to talk, let me know." It had been a long day, and I was ready to be in my own bed. "Aunt Dotty, I'm leaving now. Are you going to be okay?"

"Thank you, hon, but Billy is going to show me some of his artwork. I can see myself home." Her hand rested on his forearm. I kissed her cheek and shook Billy's hand, who barely glanced at me, since he couldn't take his eyes off of her.

As I walked to my car, I thought about the text message

Carly had sent earlier this morning. Before I started the car, I glanced at my phone, debating whether I should send her a message back. I thought about the instant attraction my aunt and Billy seemed to share, and wondered what was stopping me from giving in to my own desires.

It would be a lie to say I didn't feel those old feelings for Carly stirring inside. She was everything I ever wanted in a lover, but damn it, the thought of being hurt again scared the hell out of me. Aunt Dotty's husband had died years ago, and apparently she was ready for romance. My disastrous relationship with Frank only ended a few months ago, and I was unsure about, well, anything related to love.

I backed the car out of the parking lot, and had the sudden urge to keep driving, to flee up the interstate until I ran out of gas. When I looked at my hands on the steering wheel, my knuckles were white from gripping it so hard. Damn it, it wasn't that I didn't love Carly, it was just... oh my God.

Did I just admit that I loved her?

———

By the time I walked into my apartment building, I'd decided not to text Carly. I wouldn't leave her hanging for long, but I needed a little more space to figure out what I wanted. Plus, a long hot bath and a glass of Merlot was sounding like the perfect antidote to this very long day.

When the elevator doors opened, I detected a sweet and spicy aroma, and when I turned the corner I knew why; a huge bouquet of red and white roses was in front of my door. It was in an elaborate jade vase I immediately recognized from Carly's living room.

"You are killing me, Carly." I murmured as I entered the apartment. When I set the flowers on the coffee table, I noticed a tiny white card attached. Dread filled me. Today had been so long, and the thought of dealing with anything serious made my stomach churn. My fingers trembled as I opened the little envelope, but after I read it, all I could do was fall back on the couch and laugh.

Roses are red
I'm feeling blue
Let's keep it simple
Please, let me fuck you

I was still exhausted from our romp last night, but the thought of her doing what she'd done to me all over again made me instantly wet. I raced to the bedroom and opened the closet to find something else to wear. Then it struck me; why was I bothering? She was only a short elevator ride away. I yanked off my scrubs and grabbed a robe off the hook in the bathroom. I was going there for one reason only; sex. Before we did it though, I'd set the ground rules; no love, just a little fun between friends.

When I passed the roses on my way to leave, I stopped in my tracks. What the hell was I thinking? Remember what she said last night? The promise? I snatched the card off the table and read it through twice.

"Fuck it." I muttered, then I tossed the card in the air and raced for the door.

With an invitation like that, how could I refuse?

CHAPTER

Fourteen

CARLY

I PACED the living room in my bare feet, and the glass of wine I'd poured an hour earlier remained untouched. Ashley had to be home by now, and must have discovered the roses and the card. I'd sat at my desk all day working on that silly poem. Whenever Dad came into the office to yell at me, I'd hide it under my paperwork, barely able to focus on anything he said.

Countless sappy love poems were balled up in the trash can under the desk, and it wasn't until the day was almost over that I realized a heartfelt declaration of love was the last thing Ashley would want. I'd already ordered the roses and wouldn't let them go to waste, but instead of romantic words, I scribbled out that silly poem on the tiny white card, hoping to make her laugh. She hadn't knocked on my door, so I had a suspicion it didn't work.

Damn my stupid heart. Maybe I had to accept the fact that it truly was over between us. My stupid fantasy of picking up where we left off was just that, stupid. Ashley was a different woman than she was back then. Hell, we were kids twenty years ago. Neither of us had a clue about the real world, and I needed to admit to myself that she didn't want me for anything else but a tumble between the sheets now and then.

I snatched up my glass of wine and downed its contents. Instead of refilling it, I put the empty glass in the sink and snatched a tumbler from the cabinet. Scotch was what this situation called for.

"I can't do this." I said out loud, then gulped my drink, relishing the burn as the amber liquid filled my throat. "Friends with benefits? No string attached fling? It can't happen. There's no way I can sleep with her and keep things casual."

I was about to refill the tumbler when there was a knock at the door. I froze, terrified that I'd say the wrong thing to Ashley, and mess things up even more than I already had.

"Well, holy shit, she's either here to fuck, or to tell me to fuck off." I whispered, not knowing if I could honestly handle either of those scenarios. Paralyzed by dread, I couldn't move my feet. Another soft knock on the door, and I was frozen in place.

"Stop being such a wuss, Carly Poindexter." I muttered.

My feet finally moved. When I opened the door no one was there. I stepped out of the doorway and looked down the hall. Ashley was standing in her bathrobe by the elevator.

"Hey, you." I called out, and I was hit with a jolt of dizziness. Her face lit up, and I felt the vertigo slip away.

"I thought no one was home." She replied. A second later, she was draping her hands around my neck.

"The roses were beautiful, and the card…" Ashley laughed, "…it was perfect. I had a long-ass day, and I needed the laugh." She pecked me on the lips.

"Glad I could make you smile, Ashley. I live for…"

"Before you go any further, I need to make something perfectly clear."

"What's that?"

"Let's be friends. I can't handle anything serious right now. If you can agree to that, I'll come inside. Otherwise, I need to head back downstairs. Are you able to keep things light and simple? Because your invitation was pretty clear about wanting to sleep with me, and I'd love nothing more than to let you." Ashley leaned in and kissed the side of my neck. My thoughts raced, unable to formulate an answer, one of the few times in my life I'd struggled to find the correct words. Could I really keep things simple? My heart pounded against my ribcage, and I realized if all I could have was this, her body warm against mine on occasion, I'd have to accept it, or have no part of Ashley at all.

I stepped to the side and my voice cracked.

"Come inside, Ashley."

Silently we strolled toward my bedroom, all pretense that anything but sex was going to happen gone.

"You have nothing on under that robe, I bet." I whispered. I stood at the bedroom door, paralyzed with fear. Ashley had been walking toward the bed, but stopped in her tracks. She spun around slowly, a cautious smile spreading across her face.

"Come here and let me show you."

The muscles in my legs tightened, and I felt beads of sweat rolling down my side. My feet wouldn't budge. I was so afraid of saying or doing the wrong thing. I wanted nothing more than to make love to Ashley, but I wasn't sure if 'making love' was what she wanted. I'd give anything to make Ashley want me the way I wanted her, but at the very least, I could pretend that her heart was open to mine.

Ashley's hands moved to her waist, and moments later the cool blue fabric of her robe fell to the floor.

"Jesus." I murmured, and I felt my hands grow clammy. She stood there, head down, then raised it and our eyes locked. Ashley blushed, and I felt my heart lurch. Ashley closed the

distance between us until she stood inches away, her nose practically brushing mine. All I could think was how madly, truly,
deeply I felt love for this woman. How could I keep my feelings
out of it?

"You are so sexy, Carly Poindexter. But you'd look even
hotter with your clothes off."

———

Ashley shifted in my arms, and I opened my eyes from a
dreamless slumber. The full moon shone through the windows,
and I pulled her tighter against me, wanting to feel her soft skin
warm against mine. Then, I kissed her hair, and inhaled her
seductive scent. A strange sensation of peace filled me, coupled
with the fear that she would leave. Having Ashley in my arms
again was such a miracle, something I never expected to
happen after all our time apart. Then, the opposite of peace hit,
anxiety taking its place. Despite my iron grip on Ashley, I was
terrified of her slipping away.

"I love you." I mouthed into Ashley's back, not making a
sound. She might not want to hear it, but my mouth needed to
form the words.

Fifteen

ASHLEY

CARLY'S LIPS WERE PARTED, and her eyes were shut. The look on her dreamy face pulled me back in time to when we were teenagers. The years had been kind to Carly, but the peacefulness of sleep stripped the age from her face, rendering her into a romantic seventeen-year-old again. Damn, even asleep she looked like an angel, albeit with much more sex appeal.

I turned over on my stomach, and propped my chin up on my hands, noticing that the skin around my mouth felt scratchy and raw. The insane amount of kissing we'd done the night before was the cause, and a smile spread across my face. I wanted her mouth on mine again, and felt myself getting wet.

Was I falling in love with Carly again? Or was it just the insanely hot sex clouding my heart and my brain?

Carly shifted in her sleep, then turned on her side, where I couldn't see her face. Her back was as soft and muscular as the rest of her, and without thinking it through, I scooted into her side, and threw my arm around her waist, hugging her close to me.

"Somebody's happy to see me this morning." Carly drawled, then she turned over and the look in her dark eyes nearly took my breath away. It wasn't her usual lusty stare, but instead it was a serene gaze, filled with contentment. Her hand wrapped around the back of my neck and pulled me to her lips. One touch of her lips made me forget about morning breath, or the need to brush my teeth first. Every self-conscious protest I'd normally make, had faded from my mind with that one, simple kiss. When she pulled away, her fingers feathered over my neck, then inched into my hair sending shivers up and down my spine.

"Ashley, your face haunts my thoughts, and your eyes make me want to tie you to this bed right now, so you can never…" Carly's lips snapped shut and she withdrew her fingers from the back of my head. Sitting up against the pillows, she stretched and yawned. Her words made me smile, but only on the inside. Damn it, Carly, I needed this to be simple, but I knew deep down it was going to be impossible with her. Despite her self-assuredness, she was very sensitive, and I wondered if she was capable of keeping things casual between us.

"Carly…" I whispered, "…if I didn't have to be at work in an hour, I'd handcuff myself to the bed. Oh, and I think maybe you've been in a few of my dreams too." I murmured, then reached under the blanket, and laid my hand on her pussy, not surprised to feel her wetness. "Want to tie me up tonight?" I asked, then stuck my head under the blanket and kissed her nipple.

"Oh my God, Ashley, if you keep doing that, neither of us will make it out of this bed today. Yes, of course, tonight. You don't have to ask twice." Carly threw the blankets off. I got on my knees and kissed the tip of her nose.

"It's a date."

———

Despite the threat of tying me up that morning, no restraints were necessary that evening. Carly met me at the door buck-naked, and in less than a minute so was I. Now that we'd satisfied our carnal hunger, both of us were starving. A pizza was ordered, and we opened a bottle of Merlot to drink with it, while we devoured the pie on the balcony. Sex must have burned a lot of calories, because we ate like it was the first meal we'd had in days. Carly finished first, and then she leaned back in her chair, and gazed at me intently.

"Don't." I said, blushing.

"Don't what?"

"You know, look at me like that."

"It's kind of hard to not look at the person you're sharing a meal and conversation with." Carly smirked, then bit her lower lip. A breeze blew in and her robe opened, exposing a pinkish-brown nipple. Now I couldn't stop staring.

"Yeah, but don't look at me like that."

"Like what?"

"All siren-like, smoldering. Like a vixen ready to seduce me" I pushed my plate away, her eyes following my every move.

"I'm smoldering? Like, you find me hot?" Carly snorted, trying not to laugh.

"Remember, we are keeping this thing we have between us as casual as possible. You looking all sexy and seductive is not helping." I tore my gaze away from her, and stared down at my lap, blood rushing to my cheeks.

"Babe, I can't help it. I am Venus, the goddess of love. Looking all sexified comes naturally to me." Carly could barely contain her glee. One look at her face and I lost it.

We burst into laughter, and I realized all she had to do was stare at me precisely the way she was now, and I'd give her anything she wanted.

"Dad gave me tickets to an exhibition match at the PNC Arena for tomorrow night. Would you like to join me?" Carly reached over and took my hand.

"Um, well, what's an exhibition match? The word 'match' makes me think it's some kind of sportsball?" I'd never been a sports fan, but I remembered Carly playing on some sort of team when we were in high school.

"Yes, it's sportsball all right. It's played with a bright-yellow ball on a court with a net in the middle. Tennis. You used to watch me play back in high school." Her face looked down, but her dark brown eyes remained on me. Damn, those thick dark lashes only amped up her smoldering sex appeal. How could I say no? I nodded yes, and before I could speak, Carly's phone rang. She pulled it out of the pocket of her robe, and grimaced before shoving it back inside.

"Aren't you going to get that?" I asked, disturbed by her expression.

"No. It's my dad. He never calls this late, unless he wants to yell at me about something." Carly abruptly stood and walked inside. Moments later, she returned with another open bottle of wine. She poured herself a glass, and then her phone rang again. Carly sighed, and pulled it out. She glared at it, then answered, "Dad, what's up?"

Carly looked away, and stared toward downtown, her prior sexy look replaced by frustration. Within seconds, I could hear her father's voice yelling on the phone. Carly's shoulders drooped, and she drained her glass of wine. When she spoke, her scowl was evident in her voice.

"No way, Dad. I'm not—"

Mr. Poindexter cut her off with another tirade.

Overhearing them argue was making me uncomfortable. I

started to leave the table to go inside, when Carly's hand snaked out and covered mine. She shook her head, and gestured for me to remain seated.

"Dad, it's nine o'clock," she said, glancing at her watch. "I have told you over and over again, I've tried everything to get that deal to go through. And, no, I will not meet with Seth Blankenship this late at night. Schedule it for first thing in the morning, but I'm off the clock now." Carly's voice shook, and from the sound of it, her father was ultra-pissed.

"Dad, I'm going now. If you want to stay up all night holding Seth's hand, go for it, but I am settled in for the night. The Blankenship deal can wait until the morning." Carly disconnected the call, tossed her phone on the table, and buried her face in her hands. For a second I worried that she'd cracked the phone, but the rubber case protected it.

"Damn it, my father is a pain in the ass."

I was frozen, stuck to the chair, feeling embarrassed for Carly. From what I remembered, Grayson Poindexter had always been a hard ass. This wasn't the first time I'd heard him give his daughter hell. It was worse now than when we were teenagers, because of the woman Carly had become. If this had been anyone else, I don't think Carly would have allowed them to speak like that to her. I had a suspicion her father was her Achilles' heel. From the looks of things, she'd spent her life trying to please her father, with little success.

"I'm thirty-eight years old, Ashley, and Dad treats me like I'm fucking twelve." Carly groaned through her fingers.

"He hasn't mellowed over the years, that's for sure." I murmured, then surprised myself by stretching a hand across the table. Carly eyed it through her fingers, then reached out and took it in her hand.

"I'd give anything to have a normal relationship with Dad, you know, him supporting me like parents are supposed to do.

But, no matter what I do, it's never enough. I could sell ice to an Eskimo, an... and fuck him. Shit, I make us money, lots of it. I feel like his personal punching bag, and that's on a good day." She squeezed my hand and let go, then raked her fingers through her glossy hair.

"Why do you keep working with your father?" I asked, genuinely curious. I had no idea how she put up with it. My parents, while not perfect, were way more easygoing than Mr. Poindexter.

"Because, deep down he's a good guy, been a good Dad when it counted the most. Whenever he dials up his inner asshole, I just think back on the times when he's rescued me, and I manage to swallow my resentments and get back to work."

There was one slice of pizza left. "Are you going to eat that?" I gestured to the cardboard box on the table. Carly shook her head no. After I'd taken a couple of bites, she sighed and began speaking again, her voice different, the anger gone.

"What I wouldn't give to have a father like yours. I feel like nothing I do is good enough. I've spent my entire life trying to make the old man happy. At first, I tried to be as successful as he was. I thought building my own real-estate business and making a boatload of cash on my own would be a way to win his approval. Boy, was I wrong." Carly took a deep breath, started to say something else, then stopped.

"What is it?"

"I think he resents me. When I set up my business, he constantly ragged on it, telling me I could never be as good, or as successful as he was. That just drove me to work harder. Sometimes I just want to pull up stakes, move away, and start over somewhere else, so he'll leave me alone. Nothing I do is good enough, and I don't think he'll ever..." Carly stood up from the table and started pacing. "I'd give anything for him to just once give me credit for being good at what I do, for being a good daughter. My brother had the right idea. Dad wanted Inky to work for him too, but he said, 'hell no.' Opened his bar and kept a healthy relationship with Mom and Dad, well, with Dad anyway. Inky and Mom are like oil and water most days."

I could totally see that. Mrs. Poindexter was like a modern day Carol Brady from the Brady Bunch, if I remembered right. She and her tattooed son must not have had much in common. I rose from the table and stopped Carly in her tracks.

"Kiss me."

She wrapped her arms around my waist, and her lips grazed my neck. Carly sighed and placed her head on my shoulder.

"Thank you, Ashley." Carly murmured in my ear.

"For what?" I squeezed my arms around her tighter.

"For being here." She whispered, then Carly let go and strolled inside. Seconds later soft music filled the balcony. It was an old country song, and the woman's voice was a rich alto, her timbre melancholy as she sang about sweet dreams. Carly appeared at the entrance and started to speak, but hesitated. "May I have this dance?" She stammered, then tilted her head to the side. I walked over and draped my arms around her shoulders. Carly collapsed into me for a moment before straightening her spine. Carly's feet started to move, and I followed along, her grip tightening around my waist.

"Who's this singer? Her voice is beautiful." I whispered, our bodies swaying together in the moonlight. I felt Carly's nipples hardening through her robe.

"Patsy Cline. Her voice soothes me, though your naked body wrapped around mine would go a long way toward—"

She crushed her lips against mine, and it was like the world stopped. My eyes shut, relishing the taste of her. Carly's probing tongue explored my lips, seeking a way in. My lips parted to let her go where she wanted to go. Soon my tongue was probing her mouth too, and my arms wrapped around her tighter, holding her in place, so she would never go away. Damn, I wanted Carly, and not just in the bedroom. Maybe, if I could just accept the fact that this woman would never hurt or abandon me, I had a chance of being truly happy.

Carly pulled back enough to nibble on my lower lip, then brushed her mouth across my cheek. I slumped into her arms, and without another word being spoken, she clutched my hand in hers, and pulled me inside.

CHAPTER
Sixteen

CARLY

I WOKE UP BEFORE SUNRISE, hoping to get to the office before Dad and Mr. Blankenship. Ashley's head was on my chest, and I hated the thought of waking her up. I inhaled deeply, loving the smell of her. Hell, everything about Ashley, her skin, the thick blonde hair, her lean body combined with perfect curves. The entire package was everything I'd ever wanted. More importantly, there was the bond between us, the shared memories, and her unique ability to make me feel things no other woman on the planet could.

Her green eyes fluttered open for a second as I gently pulled myself out from under her, then she turned over and allowed me to rise from the bed. I tiptoed to my closet, turned on the light and sat at the dressing table in the middle of the room.

"Don't let them beat you down." I whispered to myself in the full-length mirror hanging on the wall. I'd barely slept last night, and the dark circles under my eyes were a dead give-away. It was strange, my thoughts while tossing and turning had alternated between dreading this upcoming meeting, and the elation of having Ashley in my bed. Then, I'd ruminated on the fact that Ashley wanted nothing more than a casual friends-who-fucked relationship, and wondered how long I'd manage to do that before losing my mind.

"C'mon, get dressed. Why the hell have I still not put a coffee maker in here?" I mumbled, then lurched from my seat to figure out what to wear. I didn't normally dress up for work, usually a simple skirt and a blouse was my day-to-day uniform, but not today. I had to dress up a bit more, because of that asshole Blankenship, and decided on a black pantsuit. Both of my ankles were in the slacks when the door flew open.

"I brought you some—" Ashley startled me. My ankles twisted in the pants and I fell forward, knocking the tray she was holding out of her hands. "Oh my god, Carly. I'm so sorry!"

I was flat on my back next to the tray she'd been holding. There was hot liquid under my head, the rich aroma of coffee filling the air. Ashley's hand flew to her mouth, her eyes wide open, frozen in shock.

"This day is turning out to be a doozy already." I muttered, then a giggle escaped. Seconds later I roared with laughter, rolling on the floor and clutching my stomach, while looking at Ashley's horrified face. "Babe, it's okay." I snorted out between guffaws.

Ashley continued staring down at me with her hand over her mouth, then I noticed her shoulders shaking.

"I can't help it." Ashley said, then started laughing too. She plopped herself on the chair and looked down at me, while I wiped tears from my eyes. Then, I glanced down and saw my slacks gathered at my ankles. I'd neglected to put on panties, and felt quite exposed.

"Can you help me up?"

Ashley pulled me to my feet, then dropped to her knees to pull my pants up as I swayed, appearing like I might fall again.

I kinda exaggerated the swaying, enjoying her hands on my thighs as she held me in place.

"What about your suits, and the carpet? Carly, where is your cleaning stuff? The kitchen?" Ashley raced out of the room before I could answer. Maybe today wouldn't be as bad as I thought. Glancing in the mirror I noticed my expression. A goofy smile spread across my cheeks, and despite making a complete jackass of myself, I looked pretty damned happy.

Ashley rushed back in and sprayed carpet cleaner on the rug to get the worst of the stains out. I'd already finished dressing, and got down on my knees to help her

"What about your clothes?" Her eyes circled the room. Except for the wall with the mirror, jeans, suits, skirts, and blouses surrounded us. I kept it organized by color, and noticed the white shirts were spotted brown now. Ashley was biting her lower lip, not knowing whether to laugh or cry. I grabbed the rag out of her hand, threw it to the floor and laced her fingers through mine.

"It's okay. I'll call the maid later, and get her to drop them off at the cleaners." I sighed, then felt my eyes filling with tears. I blinked them back, hoping Ashley didn't notice. "Ashley, thank you."

Her emerald eyes met mine, eyebrows raised. "Why are you thanking me? I ruined your—"

"Because I needed to laugh." I placed my hands on her shoulders and kissed her on the tip of her tiny, pert nose. I wasn't upset, and could honestly not care any less about the fucking clothes, or the stained carpeting. Her body relaxed into mine, and I reluctantly pulled away when I felt my body responding to the feel of her. I still had that meeting to attend, damn it.

"Babe, clothes are replaceable, and the stains will come out.

Seriously, they mean nothing to me. But you know what? The look on your face after I fell to the floor was priceless."

———

I drove around the block eight times before I could muster up the courage to park my car. After the amazing night and crazy morning I'd had with Ashley, it was wrecking my stomach to even contemplate the tortures I knew were in store for me. I'd never been so nervous about a meeting before, and I hoped I had a few minutes to go over the contracts and maybe drink a cup of coffee, instead of wearing it.

"What the hell?" I muttered as I pulled into my parking space. It was seven in the morning, two hours before our doors officially opened, and Dad's car was already there. When I stepped out of the truck, I noticed a Lexus parked by the entrance. My caffeine-free gut twisted when I saw the license plate- BLNKSHP1.

Shit.

I was being ambushed, and didn't have time to prepare myself for the almost certain tongue lashing I would receive. Dad and Seth Blankenship had been friends for most of their lives, and both were hardcore as hell when it came to business. In fact, Mr. Blankenship was more bloodthirsty than Dad, if that was even possible. He'd stop at nothing to make an extra nickel, even if that meant chewing out my father, who in turn would make my life more miserable than he usually did.

I placed my hand on the front door and froze, afraid of turning the brass knob. My eyes snapped shut, and I recalled the image of Ashley asleep, and then her laughing at my dumb ass on the floor of my closet. She'd agreed to go to the tennis match with me tonight, so at least I had something to look forward to. Plus, I'd fall over a million more times, just to see her face light up with glee, even at my own expense.

After hyperventilating for a minute, the acid in my stomach chilled out. I took a deep breath and pushed the door open. If I could have just five minutes to go over the files, I'd at least have a better chance of defending myself. Damn, it didn't matter how much I'd offered that hippy, what was his name again? Billy Turner? I'd offered him far more money than he'd ever seen in his life, and he still wouldn't budge.

"Morning, Ms. Poindexter." The security guard at the front desk mumbled, not looking me in the eye. Normally he grinned, even cracked a joke or two. Shit, Dad and Blankenship must have been bitching up a storm when they rolled up in here. I breezed past him and hit the button on the elevator.

When I turned on to the corridor where my office was located, I froze in my tracks; the door was open. Spinning on my heels, I leaned against the wall where they couldn't see me.

"What the hell am I going to tell them? It doesn't matter what I say, they're going to crucify me.!" I whispered, wracking my brain, trying to figure a way out of this mess. Then, I remembered an old parking lot that was recently put on the market. It would cost far less than The Millbrook Arms, and since it didn't have a building on it, he'd save a bundle on demolition costs. And, it was on the same block as the apartment building.

"Yes!" I mouthed silently, and crossed my fingers for luck. That empty parking lot was the answer to my prayers, I hoped. Though I could barely recall the last time I'd been to mass, I crossed myself, then walked as confidently as I could into my office.

"About time you got here." Dad barked. He was seated behind my desk while Mr. Blankenship sat across from him. That left only one open seat next to the scowling old man.

"Good morning Mr. Blankenship. Dad." I started to sit, but at the last moment decided to lean against the wall, bumping against an award I'd won hanging there. If I needed to make a quick escape, I'd be closer to the door.

"Young lady, you are disappointing me. That eyesore of a building should be emptied out by now. Have you even tried to get that loser out of there?" Mr. Blankenship's voice dripped with venom. I'd avoided eye contact with him and Dad so far, but now I had to look into his hooded eyes. Contempt was written all over his face, but his stare was especially hateful. Despite the air conditioning, trickles of sweat raced down my back.

"Sir, I've offered Mr. Turner much more than you originally budgeted. I've met with him multiple times and he refuses to sell."

"I'm prepared to make him a wealthy man. All he has to do is sign that building over to me. I don't think you've put forth your best effort. Let me be frank with you, Carly. You're a spineless wimp who doesn't know how to get things done." Blankenship shook his head, his lips curled back over yellowing teeth. "Women."

"Carly," Dad squinted his eyes "I've been riding you hard over this deal, because Seth is one of our best clients." He raised an eyebrow at Mr. Blankenship and then surprised the hell out of me. "My daughter has worked her ass off, Seth. Carly has repeatedly—"

"Failed!" Mr. Blankenship snapped. "There's no good reason why Turner hasn't signed that goddamned contract. All I'm hearing is one excuse after another."

"Sir, he's not selling, because he feels an obligation to the people who rent from him. Many of them would have no place else to go." I hoped he'd feel at least a little sympathy for the families that lived there.

"The scum who rent from him? A bunch of welfare queens and lowlifes, that's who they are. North Raleigh can support a much better class of people, people with money. That building is bringing down the value of every building in the area, including mine. And they will go whether you help me or not."

We glared at each other in silence for an uncomfortable moment. Why the hell was my father friends with this asshole? He was a heartless creep who didn't give a damn about anyone but himself. I shook my head with barely disguised disgust, and brought up the alternative property, which was a much better deal financially.

"Mr. Blankenship, recently an old parking lot on the same block as The Millbrook Arms was put on the market. The asking price is almost twenty percent less than what you initially offered Mr. Turner, plus you'd save a considerable amount on demolition costs." I crossed over to the desk and grabbed my laptop. "Let me show you the property."

"Don't bother." Blankenship's hand slapped my desk. "I want that eyesore gone. The Millbrook Arms should have been demolished years ago." The old man got to his feet. "Apparently, I will have to amp up the persuasion on Turner, since neither of you can get anything done."

Without another word he stalked out. Dad and I stared at each other with mouths opened.

"Damn him." I muttered, shaking my head. I was going to get it now.

"I don't know what's gotten into Seth. Carly, I know you've done a lot of work to make this deal go through, but could you at least try one more time to get Turner to sell?" Dad walked around the desk and placed a hand on my shoulder, startling me. I was still trying to absorb the fact that he'd defended me for a change.

"Well?" The usual hard edge crept back into Dad's voice.

"Yes, sir. I'll get right on it." I muttered, though something felt off. A voice in the back of my head screamed that something wasn't quite right with what old-man Blankenship had said. My father knew the bastard better than I did. Maybe he'd know?

"Dad, wait a sec." I stopped him before he stepped out of my office. He turned in the doorway and crossed his arms over his chest. "What did Mr. Blankenship mean when he said he was going to amp up persuasion? He'd take a loss if he offered Turner any more money."

Dad's brow furrowed, then he sighed. "Sweetie, you did the right thing offering him that parking lot down the street from the Millbrook property. Maybe it's a matter of pride?" He shut his eyes for a moment, then continued, "Carly, I know I give you a hard time, but it's because I want you to succeed. You've done everything you could do to make this deal go through." Dad shrugged his shoulders and walked out, and then he called back to me. "I don't have a clue what Seth meant."

"Screw it." I muttered, then sat down to draft yet another contract for Turner to refuse.

CHAPTER
Seventeen

ASHLEY

THE PNC ARENA WAS OLD, and about to be ripped down and replaced by a shiny new one. I remembered going to a concert here with Carly in our senior year. Back then it felt huge and modern, and I recalled feeling very grown up going to an actual concert filled with drugs, lights and screaming kids, without my parents dragging along behind me. Now it was seedy looking, the concrete floors cracked and dirty. For this tennis thingy they'd cleared out the stage in the center and erected a tennis court. Carly was in her element, blithely ignoring the surrounding decay, while her focus was entirely on the match.

"YES!"

Carly rose to her feet and yelled as a tan lanky tennis player shot the ball into the net. I'd never seen this side of her before, and I hadn't a clue what was happening in front of us. The last time I'd been to a tennis match was in high school, and only because Carly was on the team. If I recalled correctly, Carly was the victor in all the matches I'd observed.

"Do you still play? I see courts all over the city." I leaned into her and whispered, visions of her muscled arms smashing balls on a tennis court filling my head. Then, it struck me how quiet tennis was in between points. On the few occasions I'd been to a baseball or football game, the crowd had been very noisy all the way through it. Tennis was almost dignified in comparison, except for the occasional curse screamed by one of the players. Kind of like Carly—regal, but with a sharp edge.

"Huh? Oh, nope, I can't. Shoulder injury in Iraq." Carly whispered back, her jaw clenched. Obviously a touchy subject. I'd never asked her about her time in the service, because I didn't want to stir up bad memories. Maybe I should find out what happened to Carly back then if I wanted to know who she was now? My feelings had grown, and while I had a general idea of her life over the last couple of decades, I wanted to know more.

"How do you keep so fit?" I squeezed her bicep, then she bit her lower lip with those bright shiny teeth. My cheeks burned, wondering if I sounded stupid.

"I can't serve. If I swing my arm up, the way that guy is doing right now..." she pointed at the player tossing the ball in the air, "...over and over again, I'll be in agony for a solid week. I'm still able to lift weights and run, but with modified… yes!" Carly leapt to her feet again as one of the players did something very important, I guessed.

I stifled a laugh. Her enthusiasm was endearing, and then I realized this was how she lived her life. Everything she did was in the moment, her glass always half-full and not half-empty as the old saying went. My former fiancé, Frank, had been the opposite, always worried about appearances, the future, if the mail came on time. Hell, that was probably why he didn't show up on our wedding day. Hmm. Was I living my life in fear, instead of in the moment? Wondering if I could love someone and be loved in return? I glanced over at Carly, only to catch her staring at me. She placed her arm on the back of my seat and leaned in.

"What's going on? You look like you've seen a ghost." She murmured. I glanced down at the tennis court where the players were at the net shaking hands.

"I was trying to figure out what was happening down there, that's all." I leaned back into her arm, relishing the warmth against my shoulders. Carly wore a lacey black t-shirt and dyed-red jeans ripped at the knee, which was rubbing against mine. She was hot no matter what she wore, and today Carly reminded me of the tomboy I'd left behind.

"While you were figuring out the not-very-straightforward game of tennis, the taller guy won. The whole crowd got to their feet and cheered while you were deep in thought." Carly smirked, and I felt blood racing up my chest to my face. "You know, you're kinda sexy when you furrow your brows and stare off into the distance. Deep thinkers turn me on." Carly eyeballed the surrounding seats, and when she thought no one was looking she leaned in and pecked my cheek.

God, it would be so easy to fall in love with her again. My heart thudded in my chest, a wave of happiness crashing through my head. I needed to say something, a diversion from what was happening between us, because... I didn't know. I couldn't think straight when Carly was breathing in my ear like that.

"If it's over, why is everyone still in their seats?"

"Because, there is one more match to be played." Carly peeked at her watch. "You hungry? We have about ten minutes before it starts."

"God, yes."

———

"Beer or soda?" Carly asked me. A teenager in a striped uniform drummed her fingers on the counter while waiting for our order.

"Diet whatever, and popcorn, extra butter."

"Diet soda to make up for the buttery popcorn?" Carly raised an eyebrow, then told the kid what we wanted.

"You got it." I chuckled, then felt a tapping on my shoulder. I turned my head and was surprised to see Aunt Dotty.

"What are you doing here, sweetheart? I didn't know you were a tennis fan." She grinned, and I noticed a rosy glow on her cheeks. She looked happier than I remembered, content.

"I didn't know you were one either." I opened my arms and gave her a hug. "Carly, do you remember my Aunt Dotty?" I asked her when she handed me the popcorn and soda.

"Yes! Wow, it's been years. How have you been?" She placed her drink and popcorn on the counter and hugged her, then she winked at me over her shoulder.

"Wonderful, especially now that Ashley is home again. Goodness, Carly, you look exactly the same as you did in high school. I'm so happy you and my niece are—"

"What is she doing here?" A gruff voice barked. I spun around and saw Billy Turner strolling toward us. "Dotty, this is that real-estate agent, the one who keeps badgering me to sell. Are you stalking me now too?" His eyes squinted toward Carly, and his fists were clenched. Carly's mouth dropped open, then she turned to the counter and grabbed our snacks. I could see her lips moving silently, then she spun slowly around.

"I'm not selling, no matter how many goons you send over to terrorize us." The older man bit off his words, then placed a protective arm around my aunt. Her eyes were like saucers, then they hardened.

"You're the real estate agent behind all of those so-called 'accidents'? A brand new boiler and a furnace breaking at once?

The flooded basement? You are the crooked developer trying to kick those poor families out of their homes?" Her nostrils flared and then her focus shifted to me. Aunt Dotty lifted an eyebrow and stammered. "Did... did you know about this, Ashley? That she was the one behind those vicious attacks? You saw what those thugs did to that poor boy." Aunt Dotty frowned, then her gaze turned icy. I understood her apprehension, but it irked me that she'd not even asked Carly for her side of the story. For that matter, how did Billy come to his conclusions?

I thought about the building Carly and I lived in, and the undeniable wealth she'd amassed. Would Carly really hurt a group of poor people down on their luck, just so she could make a buck? I glared at her, then felt guilty for doubting Carly. I looked to the ceiling, then back at my aunt and Mr. Turner. Carly deserved the benefit of the doubt, but then I remembered that poor boy's arm, his swollen black eye.

"You're the real-estate developer that's trying to force—" I began.

"I don't know what you are talking about." Carly interrupted, "I know nothing about a little boy, or accidents, or thugs." She shrugged her shoulders, her face white as a sheet. Carly's hands were trembling, and the top layer of her popcorn spilled to the concrete floor.

"Carly Poindexter, you should be ashamed of yourself. Billy is doing the community a service, providing affordable housing to families in the area. All you are interested in is money and making it off of the backs of those less fortunate than you." Aunt Dotty was livid. "And you, Ashley James, you might want to reconsider who you spend your time with." Her lips flattened into a straight line, and then she laced her arm around Billy's and they stormed off. I turned to Carly, wondering if there was any truth to their accusations, but hating myself for even doubting her word.

"Babe, I swear, I know nothing about this. Yes, I met with Mr. Turner a few times, but I'd never, ever do anything like that." Carly pleaded. She glanced down at the spilled popcorn and mouthed the word 'fuck.'

My head was a wreck. What I needed was time to think, to process what my Aunt Dotty and Mr. Turner were accusing her of. Our eyes locked, and it was almost like a game of chicken, both of us unwilling to look away. Finally, I shifted my gaze back toward the arena.

"Let's go back to our seats. Might as well enjoy the rest of the… tennis." I tilted my head toward the entrance to the arena, and we trudged back to our seats.

The last match had already started, and to be honest, it was just a blur of flying balls and cheering fans. Carly was subdued, her snacks abandoned on the floor by her feet. Unlike the first half of the evening, our shoulders were apart, knees planted solidly in front of us. A few minutes after we sat down, I felt the strange sensation of being watched. I scanned the crowd, only to find Aunt Dotty's eyes glued to our seats. She and Mr. Turner were almost directly across from us on the other side of the tennis court. Her arms were crossed over her chest, and I felt the weight of her disapproval from fifty yards away.

I snuck a glance at Carly's profile, noticing her eyes on the floor instead of the match. She clutched the arms of the seat, and her shoulders were clenched. Misery was written all over her face, and I wondered if she'd noticed the death stare coming from my aunt. Damn it, as much as I wanted to believe her, I'd seen what those thugs had done to that boy, Hugo. His wreck of a mother struggling to keep it together for the sake of her child, and then unable to afford to buy him a little takeout

Chinese. I knew this much; Carly had never lied to me before. Passing judgment before hearing both sides of a story wasn't something I'd ever do.

I leaned into Carly's shoulder, and whispered in her ear. "We need to talk."

I pushed myself up from the seat and scooted around her to the aisle, kicking her half-finished drink by mistake. "Shit." I muttered. Flustered, I jogged up the steps to the exit. When I got there, I turned and saw Carly picking up the empty drink cup and her bag of popcorn. She trudged up the steps and tossed the garbage in the can next to the doors. I stepped into the corridor, turned and saw Carly hesitating. Anger flared in my chest.

"C'mon." I jerked my head in the opposite direction, and stomped off, then turned around to be sure Carly was following. She was shaking her head back and forth and mumbling to herself two steps behind me. Halfway down the hallway I leaned against the dirty gray wall, a jagged ball of anxiety spinning in my gut. The Carly I knew, or at least thought I knew would never do the things she'd just been accused of. But, I hadn't seen her in twenty years, didn't know the woman she'd become in the interval. I thought about the wealth she'd accumulated, the stunning artwork hanging on the walls of her penthouse. Had she made her fortune at the expense of people struggling just to put a meal on the table? Or, was I still incapable of trusting her, or anyone else for that matter?

"Carly, did you or did you not do the things Billy Turner is accusing you of?"

She lifted her chin and fixed her dark eyes on mine.

"No. Ashley, this is the first I've heard of this. Yes, I've been to the Millbrook Arms, but only to make offers on the building for our client, that's it. I've done nothing beyond that. Hell, I don't even know how you'd go about finding people to do the things he's accused me of." Carly's eyes were wet. "Whatever's happening to Mr. Turner and his tenants is wrong, and I'll do what I can to find out what's going on. But, I swear to you, I know absolutely nothing about it." She breathed. "Please, Ashley, you gotta believe me."

Either she was a very gifted actor, or she was telling me the truth. Carly stretched out her hand, palm open for me to grab if I wanted. I eyed it, wary, then realized there was no way she was behind the attacks. I trusted her, so I laced my fingers through hers.

"I believe you."

Carly slumped against the wall beside me. "What happened? I know your Aunt Dotty and Mr. Turner mentioned thugs and sabotage. What were they talking about?"

"For the last few weeks or months, they've had a bunch of accidents, and it all started when you started making him offers for the apartments." I put a finger on my chin, trying to figure out where Carly fitted in all this. "One of the children that lives there was brought into the ER after being beaten up. That's how I got involved. He caught a bunch of thugs trying to break into the building's basement if I recall it correctly. A twelve-year-old tried to stop them, and the bastards broke his arm."

"Shit." Carly ran her fingers through her hair. "No wonder Turner thinks I'm behind it. I swear I know nothing Ashley, I—"

"I trust you, Carly. I know you wouldn't... hey, your Dad—" I started, but Carly cut me off.

"My father is a miserable asshole on a good day, but that's not his style. He'd sooner cut his arm off than harm a kid." Carly paced in front of me. "Dad wants the deal to go through, but not like this. I'm there at the office every day, and I swear he conducts a clean business. We've always been on the up and up. Seth Blankenship, though, he's shady as hell, or at least I think so."

"Who's that?"

"Blankenship is the man who wants to buy the building." Carly muttered, then she stopped pacing and grabbed my shoulders. "I'll talk to Dad tomorrow. We'll get to the bottom of this, I promise."

CHAPTER

Eighteen

CARLY

"DAMN IT." I sputtered, placing the full cup of coffee back on the heated coffee thingy I'd bought to keep it warm, yet could never remember to turn on.

It was the third cup of coffee that had grown cold since I'd arrived at work. I had barely slept, and caffeine was a must if I was to get anything done today.

All I thought about as I tossed and turned in bed last night was Ashley, who'd opted to spend the night at her place, and what was happening at the Millbrook Arms apartments. It made me sick to my stomach, thinking about those poor people living there having their lives ruined by someone who didn't have a shred of humanity, only an eye for his bank balance. Plus, I couldn't bear the thought that Ashley might suspect that I was behind their misfortunes.

I gave up on sleep around five, went to the gym downstairs, then headed into work early. Catching Dad before he got busy for the day was my top priority. We needed to talk, and it wasn't going to be pretty.

Deep in my heart, I knew my father had nothing to do with

the incidents plaguing Billy Turner and his tenants. Dad would do anything to make a dollar, but harming innocent people was not his modus operandi. If it weren't for Seth Blankenship, we would have abandoned this deal weeks ago, but Blankenship refused to let it go. My gut was telling me Seth was behind the attacks, but until I had proof, there was nothing I could do about it.

I glanced at my phone, and saw that it was five after eight. Dad should be here by now, though I was surprised he hadn't popped his head in my door to yell at me already. Who knew? Maybe he was having his annual fifteen minute bout of happiness?

"Goddamn it, Cheryl, where the hell is Kristen? We were supposed to meet five minutes ago!" I heard Dad shouting in the hallway. I guessed the happiness theory was out the window, but I'd better catch him now before he got busy.

—————

"Dad, please, just give me five minutes before your appointment. It's very important." I asked. He frowned and waved me into his office.

"Carly. I'm getting pissed off about the sales data from last month and—" Dad started, but I held my hand up to stop him.

"I'm not kidding, Dad, this is urgent." I perched on the edge of the wine-colored leather couch in front of his desk. Our offices were totally different. His looked like the library at the country club, dark and oppressive. Dad rarely drew back the heavy damask curtains, and sat behind a huge oak desk. Mine was filled with contemporary furniture and artwork I'd brought from home, and the curtains were always open. I always felt like I was twelve years old and asking for an advance on my allowance when I was in his domain.

"Well, spit it out. I've got a full schedule today."

I took a deep breath. "Dad, someone is sabotaging the Mill-brook Arms apartments, and it started when Mr. Blankenship became interested in the property."

"What the hell are you talking about, Carly?" Dad took his reading glasses off and lifted an eyebrow. "Sabotage? Exactly what do you mean by that?"

"I ran into Billy Turner last night. He accused me of deliberately trying to force him out. They've had issues with their furnace, boiler, and electric box, plus—"

"That means nothing. Coincidences, that's all. It's an old property that's bound to have problems from time to time." Dad cut me off. He started to put his glasses back on, but he dropped them when I spoke the next sentence.

"A group of men beat up a kid, broke his arm." Dad's mouth dropped open. "The twelve-year-old boy caught them trying to break into the basement. These guys aren't messing around, Dad."

He stood, then circled the desk, and sat on the edge in front of me. He placed his index finger on his chin, then tried to speak, but I cut him off before he could begin.

"I think it's Mr. Blankenship, Dad. You and I run a clean business, so I hope you know I'm not accusing you of anything."

"Of course, Carly, I never thought you were." He plopped down on the couch next to me. "Seth and I go way back, graduated prep school together. He's an honorable man. I can't imagine he'd engage in these tactics. It must be someone else. Seth can't be behind this." His voice trembled. "Does Turner have any enemies?"

"Dad, he's a peace-loving, gray-haired hippie, a total throwback to the 1960s. I seriously doubt he's pissed anyone off enough they'd attack little kids. This is someone trying to chase him and his tenants out, and I only know one man who fits the bill. Can you talk to Blankenship? Maybe he'd—"

"Sweetheart, it can't possibly…" He gave a deep sigh and rose from the couch. "I'll call him. Just to put your mind at rest. Mine too."

———

The morning dragged on, and I couldn't stop thinking about Billy Turner. There had to be a clue, something that would tell me who was terrorizing him. My gut instinct said it was Seth. Dad had a ridiculous sense of honor when it came to his friends, unable to believe any of them could do something criminal. Several of his childhood buddies were successful businessmen, and a couple of them had gone to jail over their tactics. I saw Seth Blankenship in a different light. He was cold and calculating, and this wasn't the first time I'd felt uncomfortable around him. Out of all of Dad's friends, Blankenship had always been distant. At first I thought he simply hated me, but then I figured out he was like that with everyone.

"How the hell can I persuade Dad that his friend is—" Suddenly I remembered what he'd said in our meeting yesterday. That he was going to "amp up the persuasion on Turner."

"It's him, I know Blankenship's behind all this." I grabbed my phone and called Ashley. I couldn't imagine what else the bitter old man could do. Grabbing my purse, I sprinted toward the elevator while waiting for Ashley to answer her phone. "C'mon, Ashley, pick up the damn phone."

"Carly. Why are you calling so early?" Ashley yawned. "It's my day off, I wanted to sleep in."

"It's Blankenship, I know it's Blankenship who's terrorizing Turner and his residents." There was a group of people standing at the elevator, so I raced down the stairs instead.

"Yesterday in our meeting, he said he was going to amp up the persuasion on Turner, do whatever it took to get him to sell. It's gotta be him. I think he will do something horrible to those people. Ashley, I have a terrible feeling about this. I'm heading over to the Millbrook Arms to warn Mr. Turner." I threw open the door to the lobby and dashed outside to the parking lot.

"Oh my God, what if Aunt Dotty is... I'll meet you there."

———

Black smoke filled the sky as I flew into the parking lot. Orange flames shot out of broken windows, and a crowd was gathered in the parking lot, many of them crying. One woman was being forcibly held back. Two men had her firmly in their grip. Memories of Iraq flooded my brain, but I forced myself out of the car and raced toward the building.

"My son, let me go! I have to get my son!" A thin woman wailed, fighting to make the men holding her back let go. Tears streamed down her lined face, her voice ragged from screaming.

"Where? Which apartment?" I yelled over my shoulder as I raced toward the entrance.

"Third floor, 3B! Please help my baby!"

By now I'd reached the door. I turned back and saw the woman collapse into the men's arms. When I reached for the doorknob it was too hot to touch. I yanked my jacket off and used it to open the door. Smoke poured out, and I couldn't see through my burning eyes. Then I heard a man yelling from upstairs.

"Hugo!"

By now, enough smoke had escaped and I could see the stairs. I took them two at a time, then noticed they were vibrating under my feet. The figure of a man was crouched on the second story landing. He was bent over coughing, and the door to the apartment next to him had amber and orange flames coming through it. It would only be a matter of seconds before the fire would burst through.

"Get out of there!" I screamed, then the man looked up. It was Turner. He tried to stand, but fell to his knees instead. Shit, I had to get the older man out. Pushing myself up the stairs was near impossible as wave after wave of intense heat pounded me back. When I reached him, I pulled him to his feet and flung an arm around his shoulder. He was gasping for air, wet trails of black and gray soot ran from his eyes.

"Let's go man, one foot in front of the other. I'm not big enough to carry you." He nodded his head and coughed as I helped him down the stairs. Halfway down the building shook, and I felt the stairs shifting beneath our feet. Then the door of the apartment we'd been in front of upstairs blew off its hinges, sending flaming chunks of wood down the stairwell. Blinding fear took hold, and I tripped and fell down the last few steps, landing in front of the open door. Thankfully Turner landed next to me instead of on top.

"I got you!" A man's voice yelled, then I felt hands pulling me to my feet. In a flash, both Turner and I were stretched out on hot pavement. My lungs felt like they had spikes driven through them, and I struggled to breathe. Billy Turner was curled up on his side coughing, and then the sound of that woman wailing propelled me to my feet.

"Hugo! Please help my boy. He's still in there!" She once again tried to break free from the men holding her back. Sirens screamed in the distance, but I knew they'd arrive too late.

"The fire escape." Turner wheezed. "His arm is broken, he can't make it down." He pointed at the side of the building. I looked up to the third floor and saw the frightened boy's face at a window. Two windows down from him vivid red flames were shooting out. He only had moments before the fire would take him.

I jumped up and pulled the rusty ladder down. The metal was scorching hot, but not bad enough I couldn't climb up.

"Please, save my baby!"

I heard the woman screaming over the wail of sirens. Each landing of the fire escape was an obstacle course of burning plants and melting plastic lawn chairs. I kicked the plants to the ground as I charged upward, not knowing if the boy would be strong enough to make it through the smaller fires.

When I got to the third floor, the boy was at the door waiting, his arm in a sling. There was no way he could have made the climb down without help. I scooped him up in my arms.

"Hold tight!" His legs gripped my torso while he tried his best to hold on to my neck. The boy's hold on me was tenuous, with his broken arm pushing against my chest. There was no way I could carry him down like that. Shit. God knows I didn't want to hurt him, but if it meant saving his life, I'd do what I had to do. I pulled his body tight against mine, and felt his arm crunch. His anguished scream rang in my ear, and then I felt him go limp.

"Sorry kid." I muttered, his hot face pressed against my cheek. Clutching him against my torso I descended the fire escape, and when I finally reached the last flight of steps, I felt a tug on the bottom of my slacks. Billy Turner was holding his arms out for the boy.

"He's out cold!" I yelled, and handed the kid over. Once Turner had a firm grip on him he ran toward the parking lot.

"Carly! Hurry!" Ashley's voice rang through the din. Smoke was swirling and I couldn't see where her voice was coming from, then I felt a rush of heat and a roar in my ears, and the world went black.

CHAPTER
Nineteen

ASHLEY

"SO IT'S DEFINITELY NOT Carly behind all of this." Aunt Dotty said, breathing a sigh of relief. "I'm so sorry I doubted her, but Billy has been going through so much hell. I'll apologize when we get there." I'd picked her up on the way to see Billy, figuring she'd want to be there for him. I was ashamed to admit I'd had my own doubts.

"Well, unless she's warning Billy about herself, then... is that what I think it is?" Plumes of black smoke spiraled into the air from a distance. The windows were open and an acrid smell filled my nostrils.

"I've got an awful feeling about this, Ashley." Aunt Dotty's voice dropped to a whisper. She dug through her handbag until she found her phone. "I'm calling Billy."

My foot stepped harder on the gas as I raced through a yellow light. I glanced over at my aunt whose forehead was wrinkled in worry. The hand not gripping her phone was squeezing my thigh.

"Damn it, he's not answering."

"We're almost there. Let's just hope…" The words died in my mouth. It was definitely the Millbrook Arms. From two blocks away we could see it, orange and violet flames shooting from the roof.

Oh my God, Carly.

Carly was a doer, not a thinker, and if she knew someone was still in the building she wouldn't think twice about running inside. What if she was hurt? Images of her trapped in a burning room careened through my mind. I shook my head. Flaking wasn't good, and it would be too easy to fall prey to it with Carly in my head. The people who lived there might need my help.

"I'm parking a block away to leave room for the firemen." I pulled into an abandoned gas station. Aunt Dotty flung the car door open, and was halfway up the block before my feet hit the pavement.

———

A woman was being held back by two men, wailing and cussing that they let her go. Halfway up the block, my heart nearly stopped. It was Jenny Alvarez, and I knew there was only one reason she'd be freaking out.

"Lemme go, you son of a bitch!" She elbowed one of the men in his stomach, and to his credit, he only tightened his grip on her arms. When she saw me her bloodshot swollen eyes widened. She stopped struggling for a moment, and then she screamed, her voice chilling my bones.

"Hugo! Please, oh help me, Jesus, help my boy. He's still in there!"

Frozen in place, years of training in how to deal with real-life emergencies were forgotten. I was paralyzed, frantically praying Carly was okay, that she hadn't gotten here yet. I knew she'd be the first one in the building, putting her life at risk to save everyone.

I shook my head, clearing it as best I could. Jenny and Hugo didn't deserve this, the other residents who stood there in shock as their homes burned to the ground hadn't done a single thing to warrant this destruction. I scanned the parking lot, hoping to see Carly pulling up in her car, but then I saw it parked on the far side of the lot.

My heart sank.

I had to focus, damn it. People were sitting on the curb coughing and gasping for air, so I ran in their direction to see who the medics should treat first, hoping Carly was nearby, and safe.

Most of them were suffering from smoke inhalation, and after a cursory glance I knew they'd be okay. A few elderly women needed oxygen, and I'd not seen anything more than a couple of first-degree burns. Thank God their smoke alarms had alerted them in time. Then, I saw Billy limping in my direction. His arms were beet red, and his long gray hair was flattened against the sides of his face. I didn't have a first aid kit, but the sound of sirens in the distance eased my mind. Billy looked like he'd been through a war. His body shook as I examined him, and he kept glancing over his shoulder.

"Billy, your arms are burned, but I can't tell how bad they are. There should be an ambulance here any second." I reassured him, and also tried to reassure myself, but then he destroyed my composure.

"Your friend, Carly," he coughed, then fell to his knees on the pavement. "She's up there!" Billy pointed toward the side of the building. The smoke obscured my view, so I stepped forward, and the intense heat made my hands fly up to my face.

Finally, I glimpsed Carly. She was carrying someone down the metal steps. It had to be Hugo. The boy was limp in her arms. An intense bolt of fire burst through the window next to her, breaking the glass.

"Oh God, this can't be happening." I moaned, then felt someone run past me; it was Billy. He stood underneath the fire escape holding out his burnt arms for the boy. Another flare of bright orange shot out the broken window just a few feet from where Carly was lowering Hugo into Billy's arms. Once Turner had a firm grip on him, he rushed to the parking lot where the first fire truck had just pulled in. Instinctively my feet began to move, running as close to the fire escape as I could before the heat shoved me back.

"Carly! Hurry!" I yelled out. She was about to drop to the ground from the ladder when a huge boom and blinding light knocked me over. The smell of sulfur filled the air as I frantically got to my feet and searched through the clouds of smoke billowing across the parking lot.

"Where's Carly? Oh my God, where is she?" I yelled, then felt a tug on my arm. Aunt Dotty was coughing and pointing to the left. "I saw her flying through the air."

Carly was face down on the ground beside the chain-link fence surrounding the building. I raced to her side and gingerly turned her over, and what I saw ripped my heart to shreds. She was unconscious, but she was gasping for air. Placing my hands on her chest I ripped her blouse open and examined her ribcage. She'd broken some ribs in the fall, and possibly punctured a lung. I bit my lip, trying to hold back the tears. There was no way I could help her if I couldn't control myself. "Damn it, Carly, you can't—"

"We've got this, ma'am, please back away." A rough voice barked in my ear.

I swiveled my head at the sound of the paramedic's voice, then a gurney dropped beside us.

"I'm a nurse. She's broken some ribs, but I also think she's punctured a lung. I'm riding with her in the back of the ambulance."

———

"They're taking Carly into surgery now." Mark said, then handed me a cup of coffee. "I'm so sorry, Ashley." I nodded my thanks and then he patted me on the shoulder and walked away. I'd never been in this position before, in a hospital waiting room, anxiously waiting to know what was going on with someone I cared about. Never again would I not have anything except the utmost sympathy for those agonizing over the pain of a loved one.

Loved one? Did I really just admit to myself that I loved her? Sometimes it took the shock of potentially losing the one you cared about the most to realize that, yes, they were the most important person in your life. But I still wondered... it just seemed like everything had happened so damn fast. Should I trust my emotions right after experiencing such intense trauma with Carly?

The heavy sound of boots approaching caused me to look up. Carly's brother Inky was racing toward me from the emergency room entrance.

"How is she? Please, tell me Carly's going to be okay." He sank down into the seat next to me, placing his hand on mine. He was in sweats, his hair a tangled black mess. His normally cheery face was drawn, and he looked so vulnerable. I didn't know how to reach Carly's parents, then remembered we'd exchanged numbers. I'd called Inky as soon as we arrived at the hospital while he'd still been asleep.

"She's in surgery. Carly has two broken ribs, and a punctured lung. She also has a concussion, plus second-degree burns on her arms and neck." My voice rasped, still scratchy from the smoke. Inky swallowed back a sob.

"What the hell was she thinking? She could've been—" He started, but a tremendous sense of pride filled my chest. I held my hand up and interrupted.

"You would have been so proud of her. Carly rescued a boy, a child with a broken arm trapped in his apartment. If it wasn't for her, that kid would be dead." I squeezed his hand, and he sank back in the hard plastic seat.

"I'm... fuck, I'm sorry. It's just she's so fucking impulsive sometimes. Carly's the type who stops bar fights, the one who protected me from bullies when we were kids. It feels great when she does this shit, but sometimes I wish she'd back off, stop putting herself in danger. I know, I'm selfish, but I don't want anything to happen to her. I love my sister so damned much." He placed his face in his hands and let out a soft wail. When Inky looked up again wet trails of tears snaked down his cheeks. I rubbed his back, then wiped my eyes with the back of my other hand.

"I'm going to kill that asshole, and don't you dare try to stop me, Frances." Grayson Poindexter's deep voice carried through the waiting room as the sliding doors opened. Mrs. Poindexter saw us and took her husband's hand. She was dressed impeccably in a pink and blue dress, but with streaks of black running down her cheeks.

"How is Carly? What happened?" She sat on the other side of Inky, while Mr. Poindexter made a beeline for the nurses' station. Poor Mark was about to get an earful.

Inky turned to me, so I filled their mother in on the events of the morning. When I was done, she pulled a tissue out of her purse and handed it to Inky, then pulled a compact out and started to clean her face. A few moments later her jaw dropped and her head swung in my direction.

"Ashley? Ashley James? When did you get back in town?"

"About a month ago."

"Well, that explains everything." She actually smiled, then dabbed at her eyes again with the tissue.

"Excuse me?" I enquired, wondering what on earth she was talking about.

"Carly has been so moody lately. She was even short with me a few times, and she's never been like that before."

"I don't understand. What does that have to do with me?"

"Ashley James, I wasn't born yesterday. She was in love with you when you were in high school together, and I don't think she ever got over you. Now that you're back, she's a mess." Mrs. Poindexter reached across Inky and patted me on the knee. "I'm grateful you were there for her in her time of need this morning."

Inky nodded his head and shrugged. "Yeah, Ashley, Carly's got it bad for you."

Jesus Christ, had I been so blind? I knew she wanted us to become more serious, but I had no idea about the depth of her feelings. Had I been pushing her away too much?

"They don't have any news yet. I swear to god I'm going to kill that son of a bitch." Mr. Poindexter was back from harassing the nurses, and was pacing in front of us. Inky got to his feet and hugged him.

"Dad, calm down or you're going to have a heart attack or a stroke, or something really, really bad." Inky said, and Mr. Poindexter shrugged off Inky's embrace. Then he glanced in my direction.

"Why aren't you up there?" Mr. Poindexter jerked a thumb toward the nurses' station.

"Grayson, don't you remember who she is? Ashley James.

She was Carly's girlfriend back in high school. She rescued Carly today, and you owe her a great deal of thanks." Mrs. Poindexter glanced up to the ceiling and shuddered. "Thank God you were there for her."

"Oh. I thought you looked familiar. You're the reason she's been acting so funky lately." Carly's father patted me on the shoulder, then he shook his head, and grimaced. "Seth fucking Blankenship is going to—"

"Grayson, watch your language." Mrs. Poindexter clucked. Inky giggled, and I sank deeper into my seat. "Carter, stop laughing. It only encourages your father." Inky guffawed and then started sobbing again. His mother rubbed his back, while Mr. Poindexter stalked over to the nurses' station to yell some more.

Some things never changed. After all these years, Carly's family was still fucking nuts.

———

"The surgery went as well as could be expected. Carly is going to be just fine. It will be another hour or so before you can see her. She'll probably still be feeling the effects of the anesthesia, so she might not be very with it." Mark delivered the good news. "I'll let you know when you can visit with her as soon as possible."

By this time the waiting room had filled up with residents of the Millbrook Arms. As composed as Mrs. Poindexter usually was, she lost it completely when Jenny Alvarez shyly approached. I told the woman she was Carly's mother, and her eyes flooded with gratitude.

"Your daughter saved my son's life."

The two women held onto each other, both weeping for their children. By this time I knew I couldn't stay any longer. I had too much to think about, feelings to examine, and decisions to make. Now that I knew Carly would recover, I strolled over to the elevator. I didn't want to spark conversation by walking out of the main entrance, so I went up to the next floor, and left through the employee exit.

CHAPTER

Twenty

CARLY

"YOU DIDN'T HAPPEN to see Ashley at the nurses' station?"

Inky dropped my hand and laid his on my forehead. He bit his lower lip, and I already knew the answer before he could say it.

"No, but remember she works in the ER, so she might be, you know, busy or something." My brother glanced out the window, then sat in the chair next to the hospital bed.

"Maybe I should rephrase that. Have you seen Ashley at all today?" I asked, my voice flat. Inky shook his head.

"Carly, I have no idea what's going on inside her head. Ashley slipped out last night, and I haven't seen her since. I almost knocked on her door before I came today, but I felt that might be overstepping a boundary or something."

"When has that ever stopped you before?" I muttered, feeling numb inside. Ashley hadn't shown up. By noon I figured she wouldn't. I knew why she wasn't here, but I wasn't ready to face that just yet, not with my little brother staring at me with that pitiful look in his eyes.

"You never know what could happen, Carly. She could walk through that door any—" He started, but I couldn't bear to hear any more platitudes.

"Enough matchmaking optimism, okay? Would you mind it terribly if I could be alone for a while?" The last twenty-four hours had drained me, physically and emotionally. I needed space. Inky pecked my cheek.

"You got it. Call me if you need anything, or let your maid know. She can drop off anything you want from home at my place, and I'll bring it to you." Inky squeezed my hand, then left.

I glanced at the bandages on my arms, then the IV drip at my side. It was worth every bit of pain to save that little boy, but I seriously wished I could lose all the machines and bandages. The only thing I regretted was not being able to see Ashley, and I had a sinking feeling I wouldn't be laying eyes on her anytime soon.

"Ashley, what the hell did I do?" I whispered to myself. Of course, I knew the answer to that question. I'd pushed too hard, tried to rekindle what was, in her mind, a teenage romance. Ashley was a different person now, and no matter how hard I tried to bring us back together, she just wasn't interested.

I knew that I couldn't keep things casual any longer with her. I wanted it all, her mind, body, and soul. It would be difficult to give up the passionate sex we had shared, but if she couldn't provide all three, then I'd have to go back to my old ways. Problem was, the thought of fucking around with a stream of mostly anonymous women, now left me cold.

"Ha!" I laughed, then regretted it. "Shit." I wrapped my free arm without the IV over my chest. It hurt to laugh, but it was funny to think that I, Carly Poindexter, was no longer interested in random encounters. In fact, this was the very reason I'd never gotten involved with anyone since Ashley left all those years ago. I watched my friends put themselves through one agonizing relationship after another, and for what? Sex? Fuck that, I could scratch that itch anytime I wanted to, without the insane baggage of being tied down.

Tears raced down my cheeks again. All day long, even through visits from Mom and Dad, I'd been tearing up, just barely able to keep from blubbering like a baby. Mom went so far as to ask a nurse if that was a side effect of the pain meds. Thank God she said it was, but I knew better.

All I wanted was one specific girl now, and Ashley wanted nothing to do with me.

———

"Would you mind turning the TV off for me?" I asked the nurse as she prepared to leave. One of my visitors had switched it on and dropped the remote out of my reach. It was showing an old movie, one of my favorites in fact, An Affair to Remember starring Cary Grant. It was the story of a couple who fell in love, but both were involved with other people. They'd agreed to meet in six months time to see if they could pick up where they had left off. Now I couldn't bear to watch it. She was very motherly, so she plumped up my pillows, patted my hand, then turned off the television and left.

All I could think about was Ashley, and the reality of what we had between us. A couple of fuck buddies, and that was all she wanted. Hell, I wasn't sure if she even wanted that anymore. Whenever I was alone today I spoke aloud, high on the drugs, and not caring how crazy all this talking to myself must be.

"You know, Ashley, I'd do anything for you. Why the hell won't you let me in? This is insane. Why don't you want me the way I want you? Nothing beats—" The door slowly opened, and I had the good sense to shut up.

"Knock knock." Ashley stuck her head in the door. "Want some company?"

My throat thickened and I couldn't answer, so I nodded my head instead. I wondered if she was here to let me down gently, you know, the polite way of dumping someone. Or maybe this was a hallucination brought on by the painkillers? Nah, Ashley was nothing but a polite, kind woman, who had enough respect for me to let me down in person. I sighed and waited for the dumping to commence.

Ashley perched on the edge of the bed, and that was when I noticed her chin trembling. I glanced down at her hands which were shaking too. Well, at least she felt guilty about dumping my ass. Ashley's brilliant green eyes were damp, threatening to spill over. Fuck, I'd had enough tears to last a lifetime, and if she started weeping, so would I.

"I've never been so terrified in my life, Carly Poindexter. The thought of losing you made my blood run cold." Ashley breathed, then she took my hand in hers. "I apologize for not coming sooner, but I had a lot of thinking to do."

I nodded, the lump in my throat growing bigger.

Ashley turned away and glanced out the window, but her fingers locked more firmly into mine. I felt a tear sliding out of the corner of my eye. Ashley had my one good hand, so I couldn't brush it away, so I shut my eyes instead.

"I love you, Carly Poindexter. I was crazy not to own it, scared of being hurt again. But, you are the only person in my entire life who makes me feel the things that I do. I don't want to continue on the way we have been. There's nothing casual about the way I feel, and the only way I want you is if I can have you all to myself. Will you forgive me for being such an ass?"

My eyes popped open, and more tears fell. Ashley's lips parted and then shut, then she bent over and placed her mouth on mine. My lips trembled, unable to open, until I felt her tongue gently pushing against them. This had to be a dream, because she tasted even better than I remembered. Her arms wrapped around me as best she could, and I felt my chest expanding, filling up with something I couldn't name. Ashley James had just said she loved me, and she was kissing me now, and I couldn't imagine anything in the universe finer than this.

Then, the door flew open. "Ms. Poindexter, are you okay? Your heart-rate monitor is going nuts." She was right, and neither of us had noticed the insane beeping from the stupid machine next to the bed. The nurse glanced at Ashley, who was still in her scrubs. "Of all people, you should know better than to get a patient excited like that. I need you two to calm things down." She shook her finger at us, winked, then quietly shut the door behind her.

"Hey, I know it's kinda crowded, what with all these doohickies sticking out everywhere, but could you lie down beside me?"

Ashley spread out on the side without the IV, taking care not to hurt me. Once she was settled in, I said the words I'd been dying to say since she'd walked back into my life.

"I love you, Ashley James, I always have and I always will."

ASHLEY- SIX MONTHS LATER

IT WAS 90s music night at Inky's bar. Mark, who said he had exciting news, invited Carly and me, though Inky and I had a surprise of our own. Ever since Carly was hospitalized, Mark and Inky had become super chummy, so I had a feeling Inky already knew what his news was about.

We sat in the back at Carly's usual table surrounded by friends. Cameron and Marcy were there, and oddly enough, Zack, the part-time bartender was there too. Normally he kept to himself, but he was a cool guy, so it pleased me to see him relaxing with the rest of us.

"So, Carly, what's the status on the Blankenship guy? I've followed along in the newspaper, but I'm sure you know more than they do." Marcy asked, then took Cameron's hand in hers.

"He's going down, hard. Even if he escapes a prison term, which is doubtful, he's facing multiple lawsuits. Dad is suing him for defamation of character, and breach of contract. Billy Turner and the residents of the Millbrook Arms have also filed a civil suit. I'm considering one of my own, though I dare say after Dad's through with him, he won't have a pot to piss in." Carly grinned, then slid her arm over my shoulders.

"So, what's happened to the people who lived there? I read that you are helping them out." Cameron asked.

"I bought an older building on New Bern Avenue, and with some grants from the city, it's being refurbished, and then I'm gifting it to Billy Turner. He's also getting a decent settlement from the insurance company, so he can expand the apartment building if he wants. The building next door has another twenty units, and it's been vacant for years. In a way, this tragedy has worked in his favor. He'll be able to help more people down on their luck with affordable housing than he ever could have before." Carly turned to me. "I heard your Aunt Dotty is shacking up with him now."

"Yes. Billy moved into her house about a week ago. She's never been happier."

"Hey, guys. Scoot over, Ashley." Carly and I moved, so Mark could sit next to us. Inky pulled a chair from another table and sat at the end. Mark was practically bouncing in his seat, and I knew whatever he had to tell us would be big.

"So what gives?" I elbowed him. "Are you going to tell us your big news, or do we have to force it out of you?" Mark blushed, then he glanced at Inky, who nodded his head.

"Okay. This isn't just one announcement, it's several, but they're all tied together." He sipped his beer, then threw back a shot of whatever Inky had set in front of him. Mark waggled his eyebrows, and then he dropped the bomb.

"I gave my notice to the hospital today."

"You what?!" I spat out. How the hell would I get through those long shifts without my favorite buddy?

"I don't talk about this much, but I only went into nursing, because what I really wanted to do was unlikely to make me a decent living. Now that has changed." Mark took a deep breath, then his words tumbled out of his mouth in a torrent. "I've been a cellist since I was a kid, and in fact I have two degrees, the first from Berklee College of Music. Jobs with orchestras are ultra-competitive, and after auditioning around the country on every weekend and vacation I've had in years, I finally got a job offer. Guys, you don't know how long I have waited for this to happen!"

"Congratulations!" Carly smiled, then lifted her glass. "To Mark, who never gave up on his dreams!" Everyone lifted their glasses, and then a horrible thought struck me.

"Wait a second. You said you've been auditioning all over the country. Does this mean you're moving?" Damn, we'd grown close over the last few months, and I hated the thought of him moving away.

"Well, I am moving, but it's not as far as you think." Mark lifted his mug and smirked, before taking a drink. "I got a job with the Raleigh Symphony Orchestra. Inky, you tell them the next part."

Carly's brother clapped his hand on Mark's shoulder and grinned. "Well, you guys know I've been trying to rent out the space next door for a couple of years now. Mark is not only becoming a famous musician, the two of us are opening a coffee shop and bookstore next door, and he will live upstairs from it!"

"Oh, thank God! That's so awesome!" I breathed a sigh of relief. Having Carly back in my life was the best gift the universe had ever given me, but my friendship with Mark meant a lot too. Despite Raleigh being my hometown, I didn't know that many people yet. Mark and everyone else at this table had come to mean a lot to me over the past few months.

"Oh, and before we finish all these congratulations, there is one more announcement." Mark gestured across the table toward Zack. "Meet the new manager of Jacked Up Coffee And Books, Zack Bronstein."

Zack blushed and grinned from ear to ear. It looked like lots of changes were in store for our group of friends. I glanced over at Carly, then at Inky. He mouthed, "Are you ready?" I subtly nodded, and he got up from the table and raced over to the DJ. A minute later the song changed, and it just so happened to be the song Carly and I had come to call our own. We'd spent many nights on her balcony swaying in each other's arms to Truly Madly Deeply by Savage Garden. I looked over at her and a small smile danced across her face.

"May I have this dance?" I whispered in her ear.

"I would never pass up a chance to hold you in my arms. After you."

Mark stood to let us pass, then I took Carly's hand and led her to the makeshift dance floor, which we had all to ourselves. She wrapped her arms around my waist and pulled me in tight. As always, I inhaled deeply, relishing her clean floral scent.

"Every time we dance to this song, I think about how close we were to losing each other. I never want to spend a day without you by my side, Carly Poindexter." I breathed in her ear. She pulled me in closer, placing a hand on that in-between place that wasn't quite my back, and also wasn't my ass. I loved it when she touched me there.

"You are so luscious." I whispered in her ear, then I nibbled on her earlobe and she fell into me for just a quick moment. I snuck a glance over to our table. Inky was rolling his hands in a circle with a look on his face telling me to hurry. I never thought this day would come, and suddenly I was petrified. What if...? Damn it, just do it already.

"Carly?"

"Yes?"

I reached behind me and removed her hands from my back. Her eyes squinted, and she started to say something, but stopped. I dropped to my knees in front of her, and she looked even more perplexed. The DJ cut the music off and the bar grew silent.

"Carly Poindexter, you are the most stubborn and lovable woman I've ever known. When I first met you, I was so empty inside, afraid of feeling anything, numb in fact. You've changed that for me. Now I have something beating in my chest again. You're rewritten my heart, and I want to let the future in, but only if you're in it. I can't imagine living another day without you, and I feel like we were robbed of too many years already." The room grew blurry for a moment, and I forced myself to keep speaking. "Will you marry me? I know I should have discussed this with you earlier, but I'm too impatient to wait. I can't imagine anything else I want more than having you with me every day for the rest of my life." My heart was galloping a mile a minute. When I looked up, tears were streaming down Carly's cheeks, then she reached for my hand and pulled me to my feet. She reached into her jean's pocket and pulled out a small, velvet box.

"Damn it, of course I'll marry you, Ashley. Um, it's kind of funny, but I bought this for you yesterday, and I was waiting for the right time to give it to you." She swiped at her eyes. "I guess this is as good a time as any." Carly opened the box and took my hand in hers, then slid the most stunning ring on my finger. An emerald, with a pearl on each side of it.

Shit, now it was my turn to blubber. I could barely see anything through my tears, and I wondered at the beauty of this woman, the one I'd done my best to keep at arm's length.

Carly's lips crashed against mine, and the usual high I got from kissing her was magnified by a thousand, at least. My legs shook, and I was afraid I'd fall to the floor. Then, I broke the kiss, and we faced the bar where every patron was cheering us on. Carly's eyes grew wide and she glanced around the room, almost as if she'd forgotten anyone else was there.

A huge smile spread across her face, then she gave an embarrassed little wave, and whispered in my ear, "I love you, Ashley."

———

Thank you for reading Ashley and Carly's love story, and I hope you enjoyed it. Follow Tessa Vidal on Bookbub to know about her books and when there are new releases.

———

Here's an excerpt from an earlier novel, Crave. It's the love story between Simona and Amber.

———

"Mr. Werther, this is a first edition Gore Vidal, *The City and the Pillar*. Oh, and it's signed by the author and in superb condition. Do you want me to hold it for you?" I asked over the phone while Christy refilled my coffee. She spilled a little, and I jerked in response. I was about to shoo her away, but a huge grin spread across her face. It was the first smile I had seen from her since Kathryn gave us the bad news.

"I'm sorry, sir, I didn't get that. It's 50% off. Okay. Well, call me back if you change your mind. Have a good day." I hung up, wondering what the hell had gotten into Christy. She was bouncing up and down.

"You need to come out front right now." She winked.

"Why?"

"Because a tall, dark-haired Goddess just walked in, and

she's worth ogling." Christy practically ran out of the stockroom door, before stopping to regain her composure. She turned back and faced me.

"Come on, seriously, you don't want to miss this." She licked her lips and walked out to the sales floor. Normally we didn't gawk at the customers. She was happily married, and me, well, I just wasn't the type of girl who ever got lucky. I always thought, why bother? She must have been something special to impress her this much. I got up from the desk and followed, curiosity getting the best of me.

I peeked out the door and saw no one. We'd only opened a few minutes ago, and the shop appeared empty.

I stared at Christy, who was standing midway up the aisle. Was she *polishing* a book?

What the hell? I raised my eyebrows. She discreetly dipped her head in the direction of the rare books room, grinned and winked.

I strolled up the aisle and tripped over my feet, almost knocking her over. The blood rushed to my face, hoping whoever the customer was didn't notice. Christy giggled, then not so subtly pointed. I gently slapped her index finger down, then ventured a glance into the room.

A very tall woman with short, wavy black hair had her back to us while turning a book over in her hands. Thankfully, she didn't see us make stupid fools of ourselves. I shrugged my shoulders at Christy, prepared to walk back to the stockroom and start emailing and calling customers again. Then she turned around.

Both Christy and I stood there, mouths open as the woman faced us. Blood rushed to my face, embarrassed for being caught gawking. The woman's face broke into a huge grin. Her perfect white teeth were like headlights in the dark shop.

"Are you Amber? I got an email from you earlier, telling me about a going out of business sale."

My heart galloped, then slowed down as I forced my lips to move. I tentatively raised my left hand in a half-wave.

"That would be me. I'm Amber. I, um, sent the emails." Shit, I sounded like an idiot. *Pull yourself together.* She was a raven haired beauty queen and I was an out of shape nerd she'd never look twice at.

She sauntered over, holding out her hand.

"I'm Simona Hernandez. I've bought a lot from you over the years, though I don't often get to come here myself. It's nice to meet you." She said, an amused smile gracing her face. I shook her hand, nervous about my sweaty palms. I snuck a glance at Christy who was still polishing the book, her mouth wide open. I elbowed her.

"Oh, I'm sorry. I'm Christy. I work here too." She said, then she dropped the book on the shelf next to her and shook her hand. Her neck was flushed, her makeup diffusing the redness of her face. At least she had the decency to be embarrassed. The two of us were being very unprofessional. I cleared my throat, then spoke.

"It's nice to meet you. You're one of our best customers, and we're glad to be offering you some great deals on our inventory." Wouldn't you know it, she was the most stunning woman to set foot in the store and *now* we were closing?

"Please, call me Simona. Books are my escape, always have been. When I discovered rare and collectible books, it was like an entire world opened up that I hadn't known existed." She leaned against the wall behind her. I fully expected the building to shift as she settled against it. Only a Goddess could do that.

Pull yourself together Amber.

"I'll be back in a moment, I need to get something from the office. Would you like some coffee?" I asked.

"No, I just came from the coffee shop up the street, but thanks for the offer." She replied, then turned to examine the books on the shelf next to her.

I hurried down the aisle, forcing myself not to turn around for another glimpse. When I got to the stockroom, I rifled through the stack of paper on my desk, eager to find the printouts I'd made for our preferred customers. Fuck, where the hell was it? Finally I saw the bright yellow sticky note with her name on it. I ripped it off the stack of stapled paper, then sank in my chair for a moment.

Be professional. Yes, she's attractive, but she's the type of attractive you can only dream about. Just do your job with a little dignity, okay?

I pushed myself out of my seat and took a deep breath, opened the stockroom door and walked out to find Christy being, well, *Christy*.

Simona was leaning against the wall, her eyebrows pulled together with a look of embarrassment. Christy was polishing that damn book again, a blank look on her face while she stared without shame. She apparently thought rubbing the book would distract our customer from her ogling.

Not working sweetheart.

"Christy, could you, um, make some more coffee? I forgot to put on another pot while I was in the back." I asked, hoping to spare Simona her lustful, very obvious gaze.

"Yeah I, I can do that." She stumbled to the stockroom, allowing herself one last look. Finally the door closed behind her.

"I'm so sorry, I don't know what's gotten into her. Normally she's..."

"Don't worry about her." She said. Her full lips turned up once more with that brilliant smile. "So why is the shop closing? It can't be because of slow sales. It's always busy when I call, and I know if I'm purchasing a lot here, others must be as well."

"Bartholomew passed away, and his widow wants to move on. Too many bad memories, or perhaps I should say good ones. She's liquidating everything and moving out of town." I had come to grips with the situation, but only enough not to break down in tears at work. I selfishly wished she would let Christy and I run it. Nothing would change her mind.

"I'm so sorry to hear that; what a sad ending to such a lovely place." Then she came to the point of her visit. "So, what's for sale?"

My mind blanked for just a second, then I remembered the printouts in my hand. I held them out to her.

"This is a list of all of your prior purchases. There is also a list of all the rare books we still have in stock. I took the liberty of compiling a list of titles I thought you'd personally be interested in." My voice was steady now that I could focus on work instead of, well, *her*.

She glanced through the reports with interest. It was easy to come up with titles I thought she'd like. She usually bought my personal favorites, typically witty writers like Henry James, Vidal, or Evelyn Waugh.

"This is amazing, no wonder I've spent so much money here. You really know my tastes very well." Simona laughed, her eyes glued to the sheets of paper.

"To be honest, it was super easy to come up with since I like the same writers you do. Also, I've noticed that as a collector you still purchase books I'm assuming you like to read. Many people stick them on a shelf to increase in value. Am I correct?" I asked, excitement creeping into my voice.

"You're right on the money. I mean, I treat my books with the utmost care and respect, but I actually do read and enjoy them." Her eyes moved up and down the list scanning the titles

I'd selected. I loved finding someone who enjoyed reading their books instead of sticking them in an airtight container. Most collectors didn't bother to read, treating them more like stocks or bonds. She looked up from the pages, her golden brown eyes boring straight into mine.

"You must love working here. I'm so sorry you will be leaving what should be your career. You've got a gift for this. I'll admit to a certain selfishness, but I will miss having your phone calls and emails. You always make the best choices for my library." I could see her being intimidating to most people, but her words struck a chord in me. True appreciation from one book lover to another.

"Thank you." I looked away. Her gaze was intense. I turned to the surrounding books, needing to get my focus back on the subject at hand.

"If you don't mind, I'm going straight home to compare your recommendations with what's already on my shelves, since I do occasionally shop with other dealers." She put her hand out for me to shake. I grasped it, her skin warm and dry.

"I look forward to hearing from you soon." I breathed.

When she got to the front door, she turned around.

"Call me Simona, please." She grinned, then slipped out the door. My heart raced as I watched her descend the steps. Oh, if only she was into nerds who rarely saw the sun.

I turned around and nearly ran into Christy who'd snuck up behind me.

"Oh my God, Amber, was I right or what? She is so freaking..." Her words died in her throat as I heard the front door open once more. It was her, Simona.

"Miss, I'm sorry, I forgot your name. May I have a word alone with Amber?" She asked Christy. She had the good grace to nod and walk back to the stockroom. Once the door closed, I turned around to face her.

"I thought about something on my way to the car…"

"Sure, what can I help you with? Did you have a question about the suggestions I made for you?" I murmured, happy just to speak with her again.

She grabbed one of my hands in hers. Damn it, I could feel my palms slicking up again. Thoughts raced through my mind, none based in reality. There was no way she'd ever be interested in me. I swore she was going to ask me out on a…

"Do you have a job lined up after the bookstore closes? My personal assistant just quit on me, and I really need someone I can count on. You're organized, and you've impressed me over the phone and in emails for months. Now that I've met you, I think you'll be a great fit." Simona spoke fast, almost too fast for me to register her words.

"I, um, I don't have a job lined up yet, but I know I'm going to need one." I stammered. This might not be a dream date, but a job would be nice too.

She looked at me expectantly, I guess wanting me to accept the job on the spot. It was tempting, very tempting. Finally, she spoke.

"You don't have to say yes right away, I mean obviously you need to know more. Let me tell you about…" Her eyes closed, then she reached into her back pocket and pulled out her phone which was vibrating. She glanced at it then continued.

"This is why I need an assistant, because my life is very busy. My first day off in months and, damn it, I'm sorry, an emergency has come up. Can I email you the job description, and salary? I feel like we've already conducted a very lengthy interview, and I know I want to hire you." Her face rearranged itself from vibrant to grim. I noticed a few strands of gray woven through her dark, tousled hair.

"Please do, you can use my work email. My boss won't mind." I felt my pulse pounding in my ears.

She took my sweaty palm in her dry one and shook it once more. I swore she held onto it a beat longer than normal.

"Thanks." She slowly walked out the door, turning around to give me a little wave as she left. She looked exhausted now. When I first saw her she'd looked so lighthearted, vibrant, full of energy.

"AMBER! Oh my God!" Christy shrieked.

I jumped, then felt her hug me from behind. She'd been eavesdropping the whole time.

"If you don't take that job I will personally escort you to the nearest mental health clinic." She said.

"Well, I don't want my sanity on your conscience." I nodded my head, turned around, and hugged her back.

I'd be crazy not to take it, right?

———

Want to read more of Simona and Amber's story? The full novel Crave is available at your favorite bookstore.

Tessa Vidal is a feel-young woman in her fifties who lives for romance. A church secretary by day, Tessa writes romantic tales of love at night about women defying boundaries and forging relationships that stand the test of time.